MAY 09 2014

P9-BZY-788

WITHDRAWN
MUSSER PUBLIC LIBRARY

MUSSER PUBLIC LIBRARY
MUSCATINE, IA 52761

THE MOONLIT ROAD

Adapted by
Vincent Goodwin

Illustrated by
Rod Espinosa

Based upon the works of
Ambrose Bierce

magic
Wagon

visit us at
www.abdopublishing.com

Published by Magic Wagon, a division of the ABDO Group, PO Box 398166, Minneapolis, MN 55439. Copyright © 2014 by Abdo Consulting Group, Inc. International copyrights reserved in all countries. All rights reserved. No part of this book may be reproduced in any form without written permission from the publisher.

Graphic Planet™ is a trademark and logo of Magic Wagon.

Printed in the United States of America, North Mankato, Minnesota.
102013
012014
This book contains at least 10% recycled materials.

Original story by Ambrose Bierce
Adapted by Vincent Goodwin
Illustrated by Rod Espinosa
Colored and lettered by Rod Espinosa
Edited by Stephanie Hedlund and Rochelle Baltzer
Interior layout and design by Antarctic Press
Cover art by Rod Espinosa
Cover design by Neil Klinepier

Library of Congress Cataloging-in-Publication Data

Goodwin, Vincent, author.
  The moonlit road / adapted by Vincent Goodwin ; illustrated by Rod Espinosa.
     pages cm. -- (Graphic horror)
  "Based upon the works of Ambrose Bierce."
  Summary: In this graphic version of the story by Ambrose Bierce, Joel Jr. arrives home to find that his mother has been strangled--what follows is told from the perspective of Joel Jr., his father, and his mother's ghost.
  ISBN 978-1-62402-016-2
1. Bierce, Ambrose, 1842-1914? Moonlit road--Adaptations. 2. Murder--Comic books, strips, etc. 3. Murder--Juvenile fiction. 4. Ghost stories. 5. Horror tales. [1. Graphic novels. 2. Bierce, Ambrose, 1842-1914? Moonlit road--Adaptations. 3. Ghosts--Fiction. 4. Murder--Fiction. 5. Horror stories.] I. Espinosa, Rod, illustrator. II. Bierce, Ambrose, 1842-1914? Moonlit road. III. Title.
  PZ7.7.G66Mo 2014
  741.5'973--dc23   2013025319

TABLE OF CONTENTS

3 0088 00049 3436

MAY 09 2014

MUSSER PUBLIC LIBRARY
MUSCATINE, IA 52761

THE MOONLIT ROAD

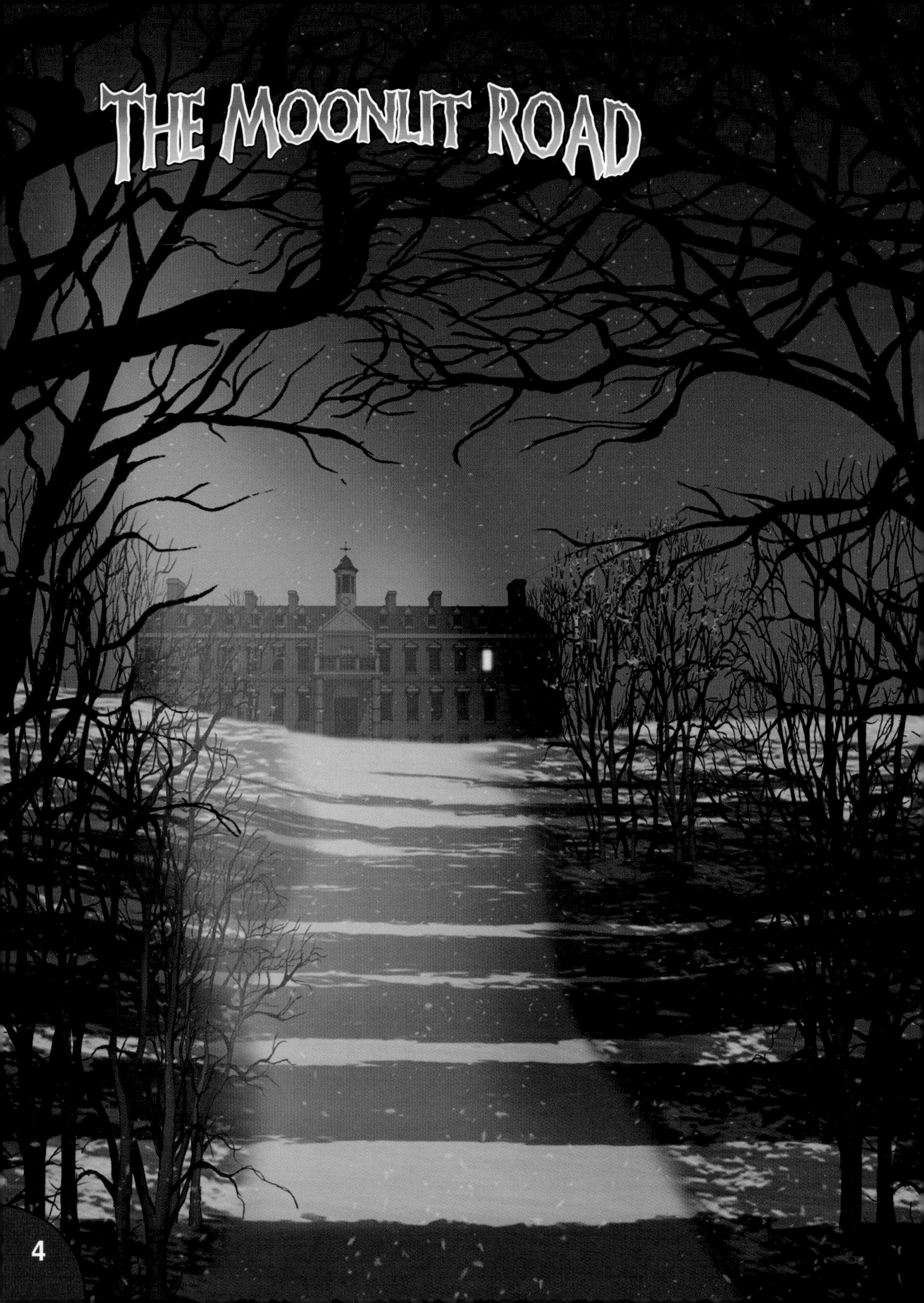

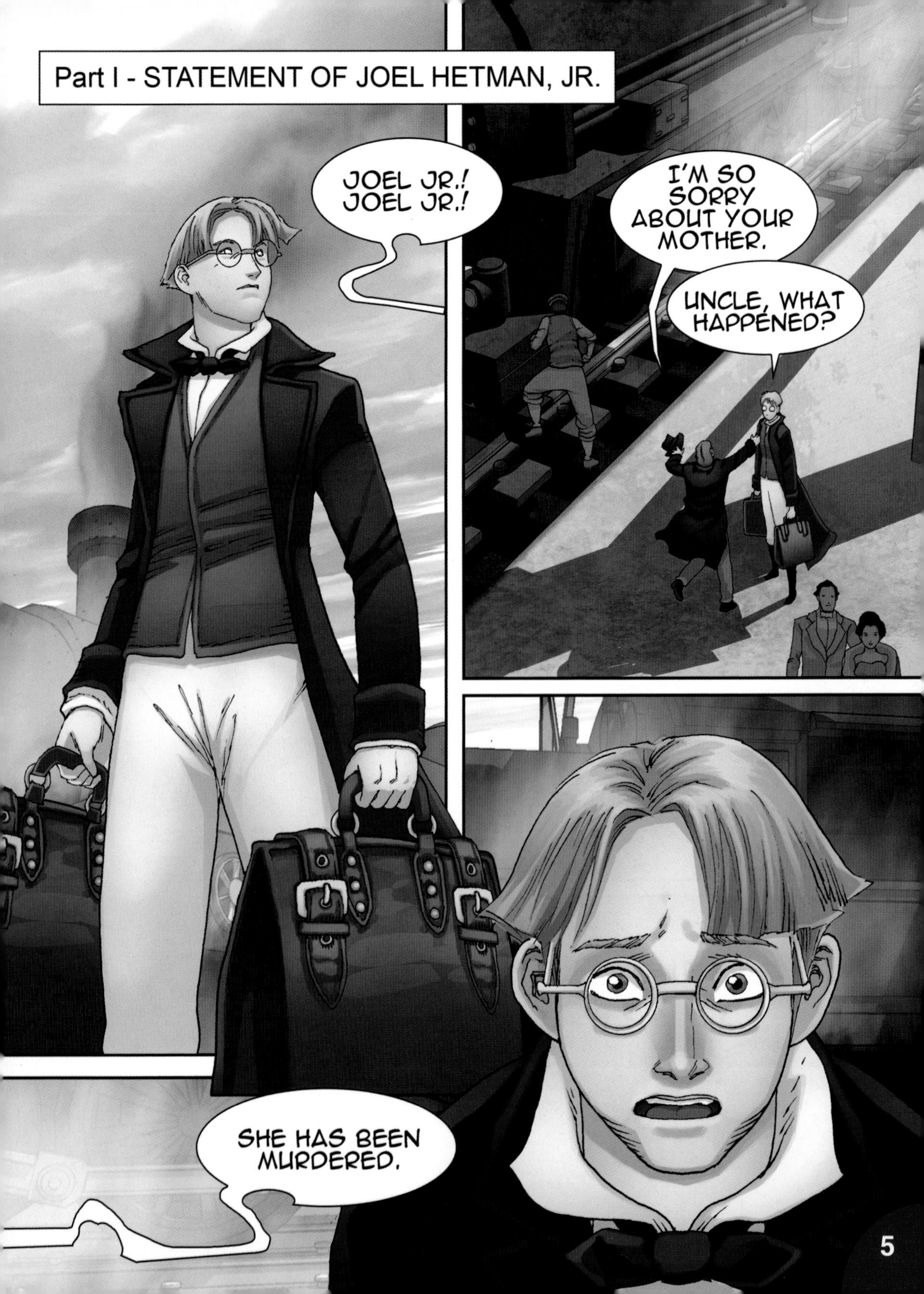
Part I - STATEMENT OF JOEL HETMAN, JR.
JOEL JR.! JOEL JR.!
I'M SO SORRY ABOUT YOUR MOTHER.
UNCLE, WHAT HAPPENED?
SHE HAS BEEN MURDERED.

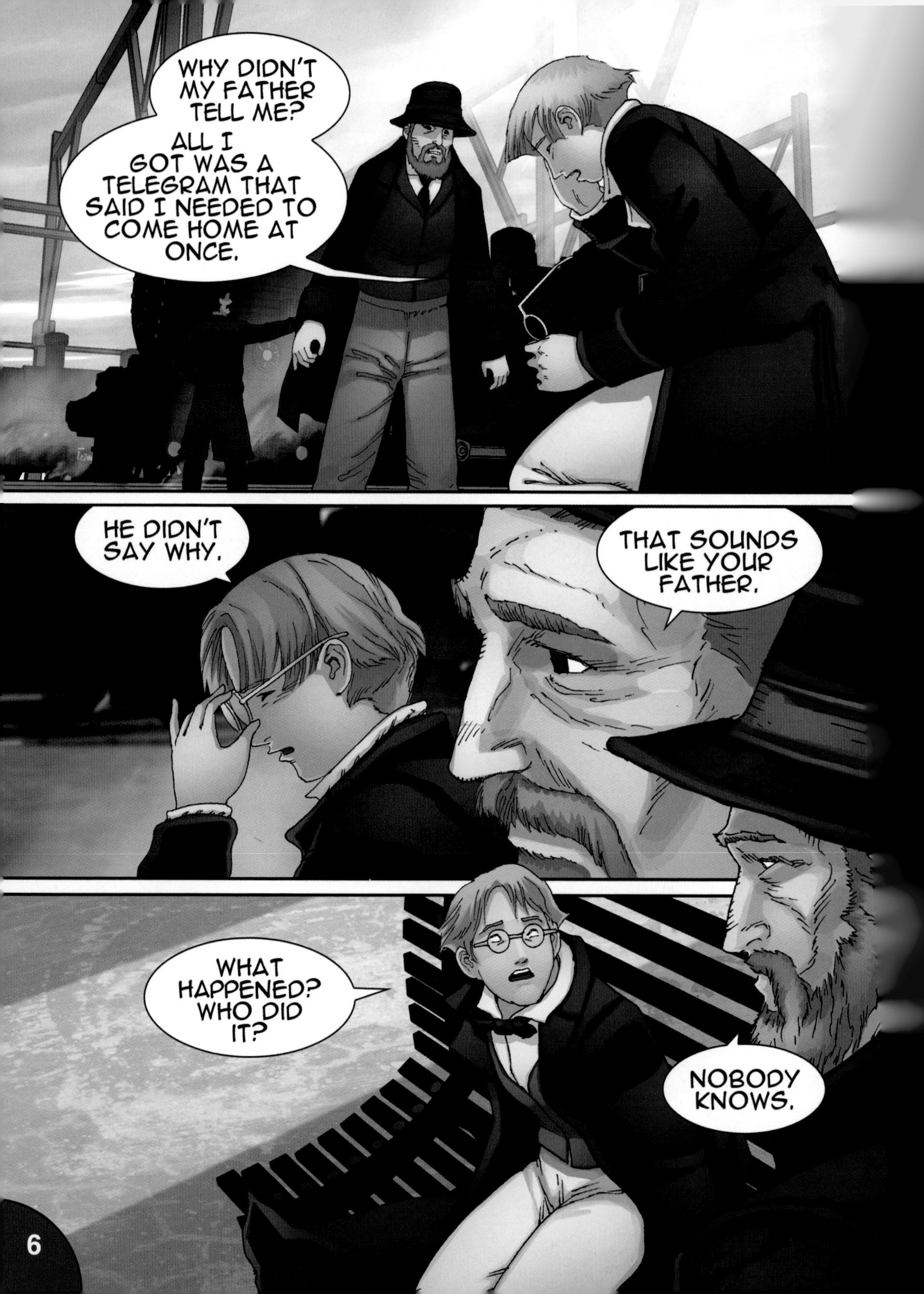
WHY DIDN'T MY FATHER TELL ME?
ALL I GOT WAS A TELEGRAM THAT SAID I NEEDED TO COME HOME AT ONCE.
HE DIDN'T SAY WHY.
THAT SOUNDS LIKE YOUR FATHER.
WHAT HAPPENED? WHO DID IT?
NOBODY KNOWS.

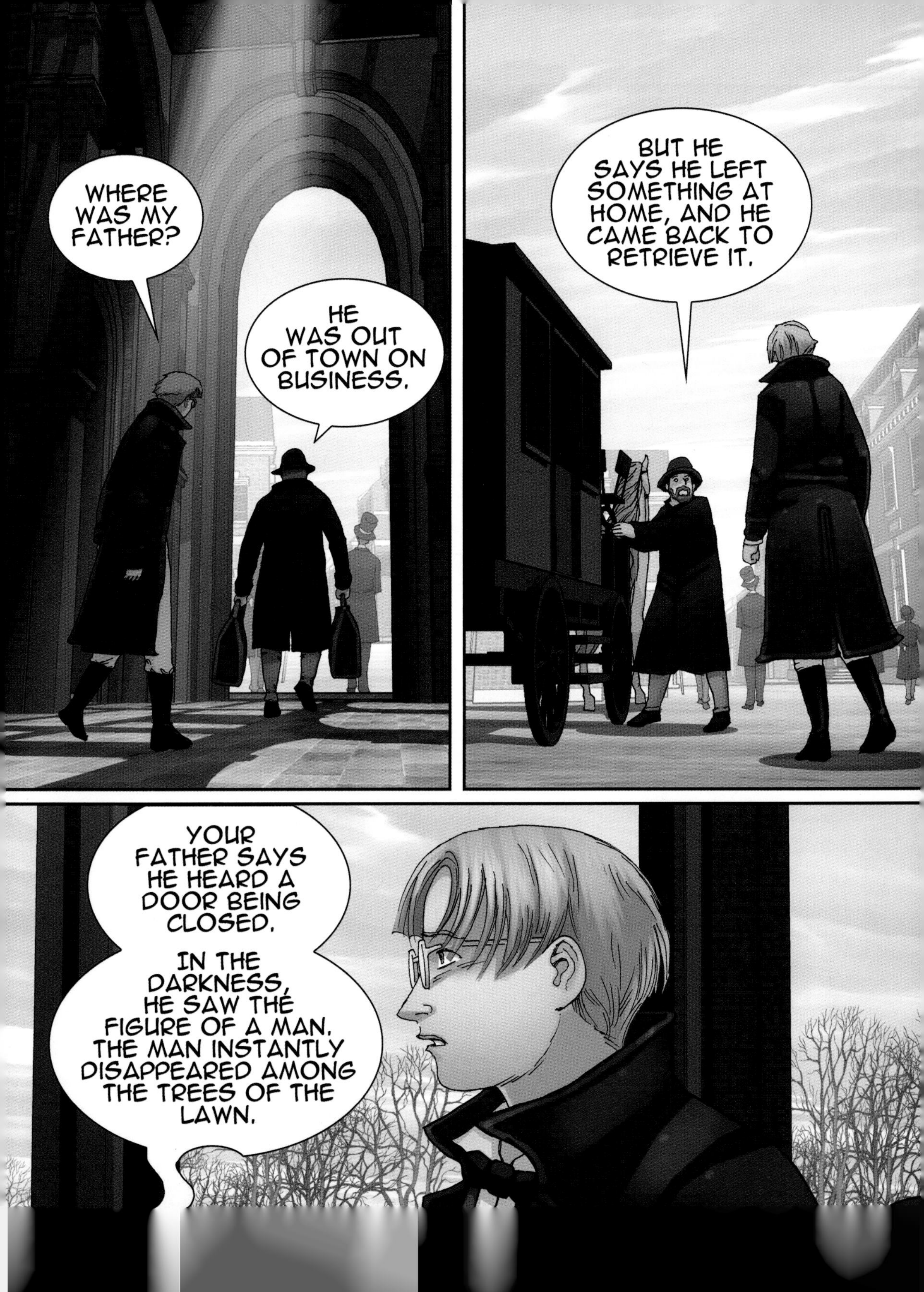
WHERE WAS MY FATHER?
HE WAS OUT OF TOWN ON BUSINESS.
BUT HE SAYS HE LEFT SOMETHING AT HOME, AND HE CAME BACK TO RETRIEVE IT.
YOUR FATHER SAYS HE HEARD A DOOR BEING CLOSED.
IN THE DARKNESS, HE SAW THE FIGURE OF A MAN. THE MAN INSTANTLY DISAPPEARED AMONG THE TREES OF THE LAWN.

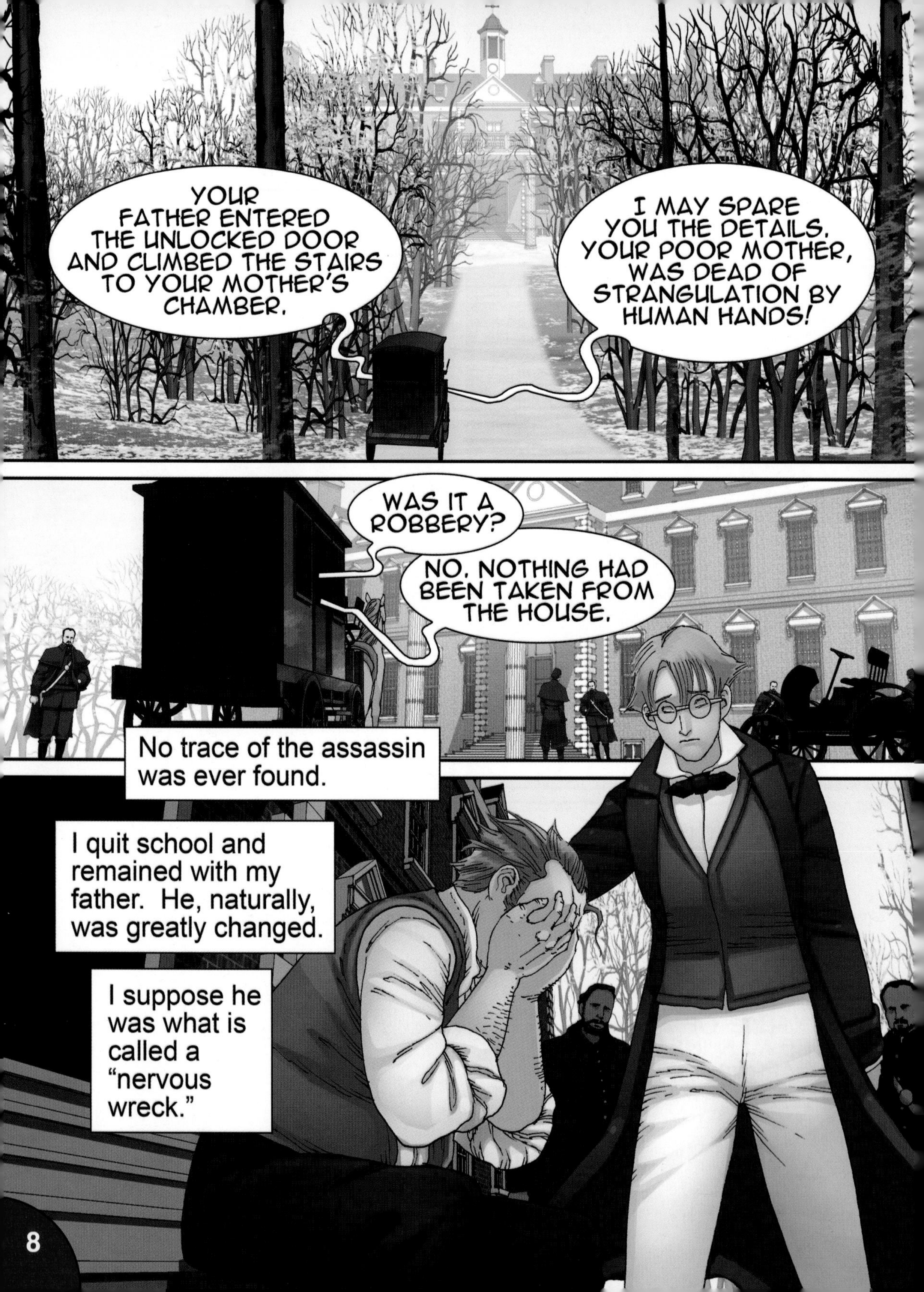
YOUR FATHER ENTERED THE UNLOCKED DOOR AND CLIMBED THE STAIRS TO YOUR MOTHER'S CHAMBER.
I MAY SPARE YOU THE DETAILS. YOUR POOR MOTHER, WAS DEAD OF STRANGULATION BY HUMAN HANDS!
WAS IT A ROBBERY?
NO. NOTHING HAD BEEN TAKEN FROM THE HOUSE.
No trace of the assassin was ever found.
I quit school and remained with my father. He, naturally, was greatly changed.
I suppose he was what is called a "nervous wreck."

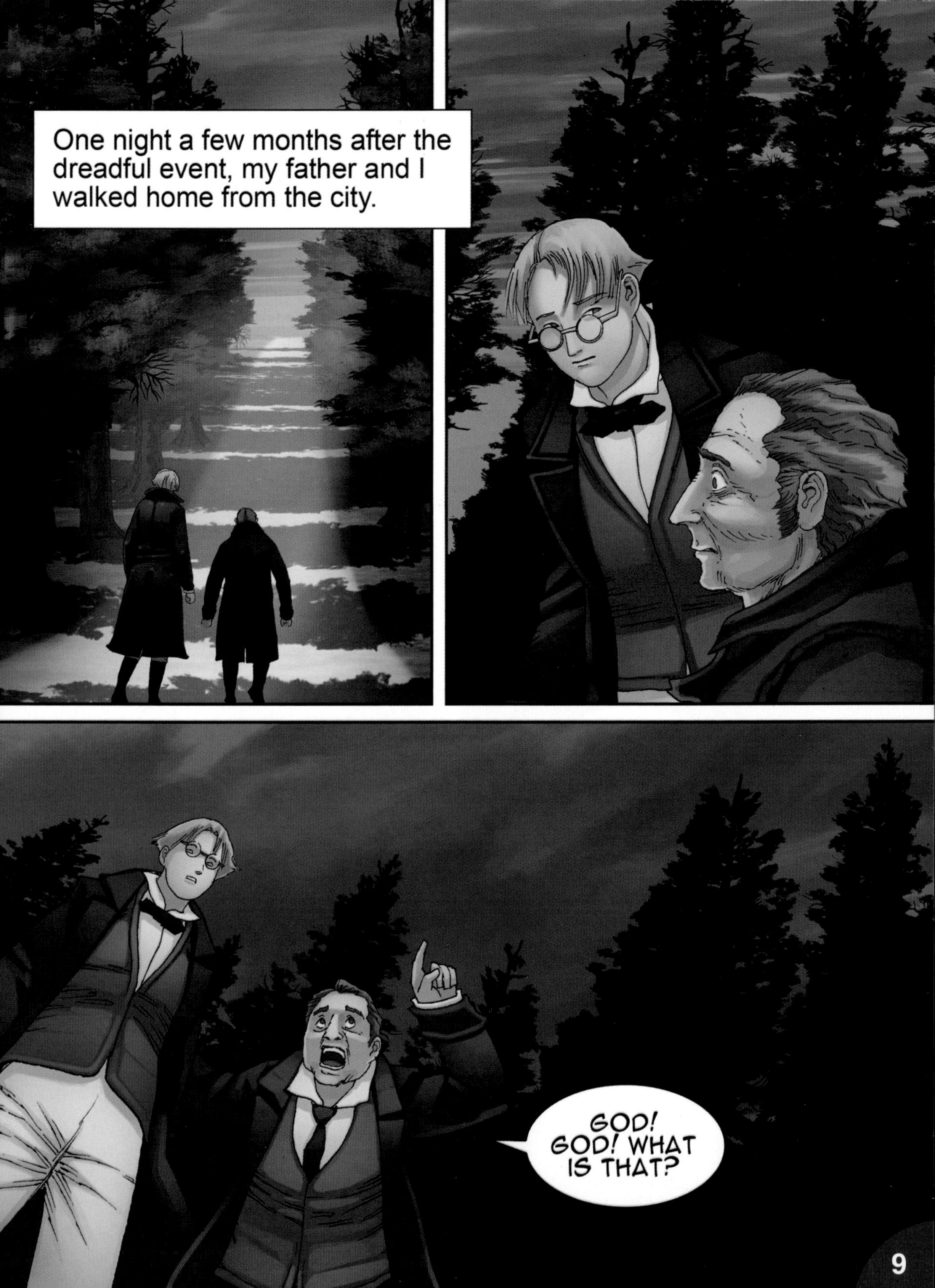
One night a few months after the dreadful event, my father and I walked home from the city.
GOD! GOD! WHAT IS THAT?

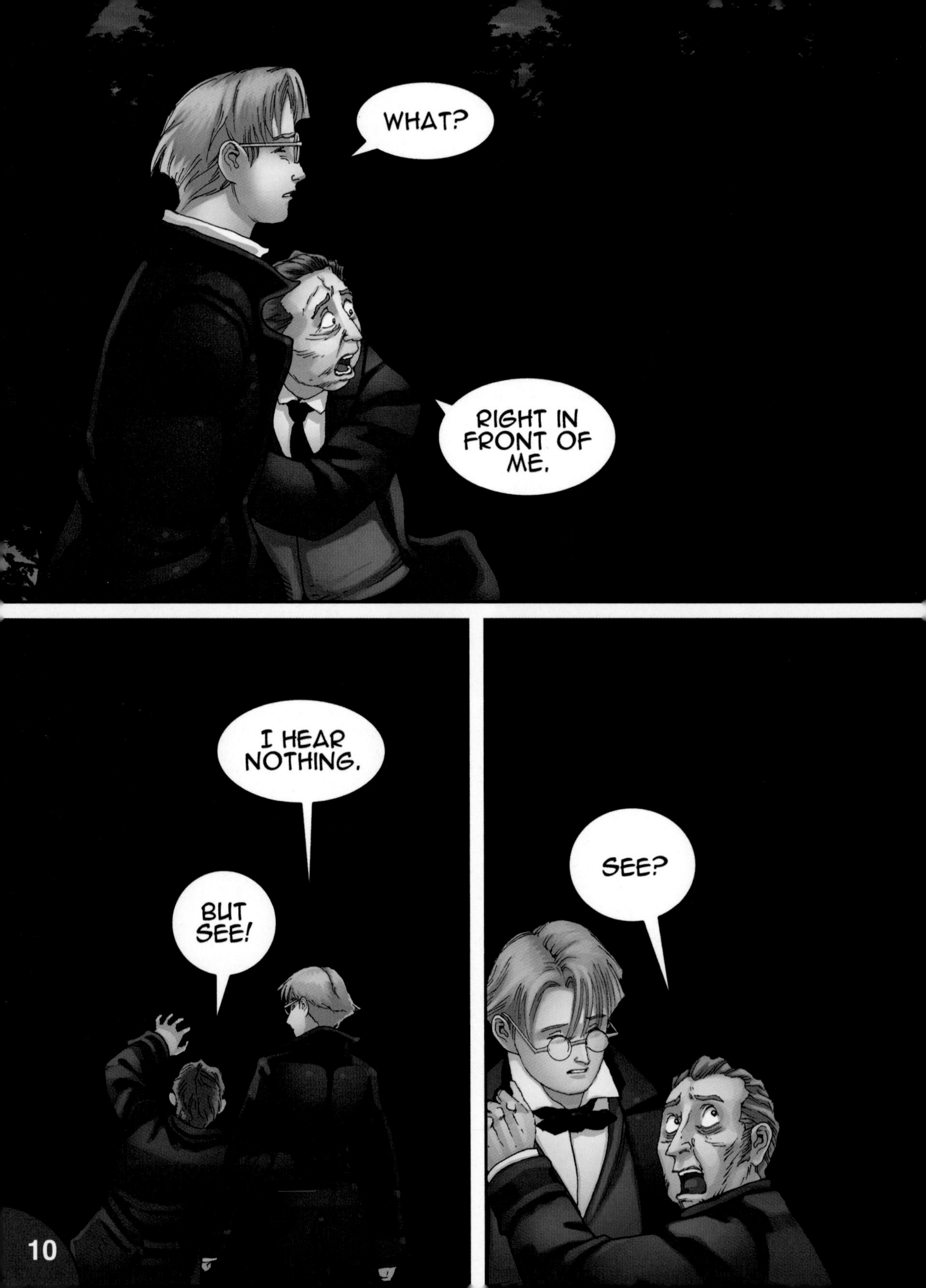
WHAT?
RIGHT IN FRONT OF ME.
I HEAR NOTHING.
BUT SEE!
SEE?

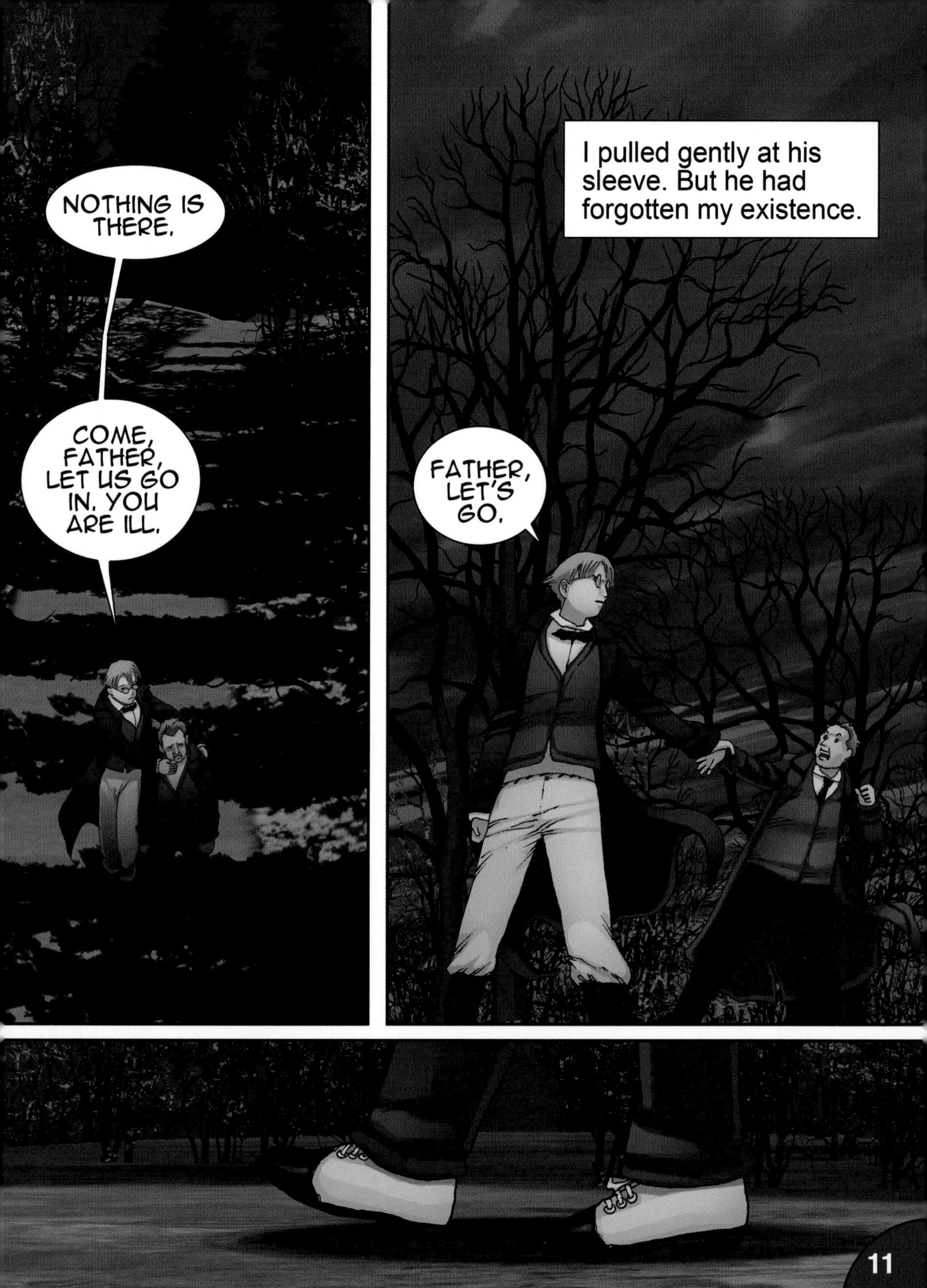
NOTHING IS THERE.
COME, FATHER, LET US GO IN. YOU ARE ILL.
I pulled gently at his sleeve. But he had forgotten my existence.
FATHER, LET'S GO.

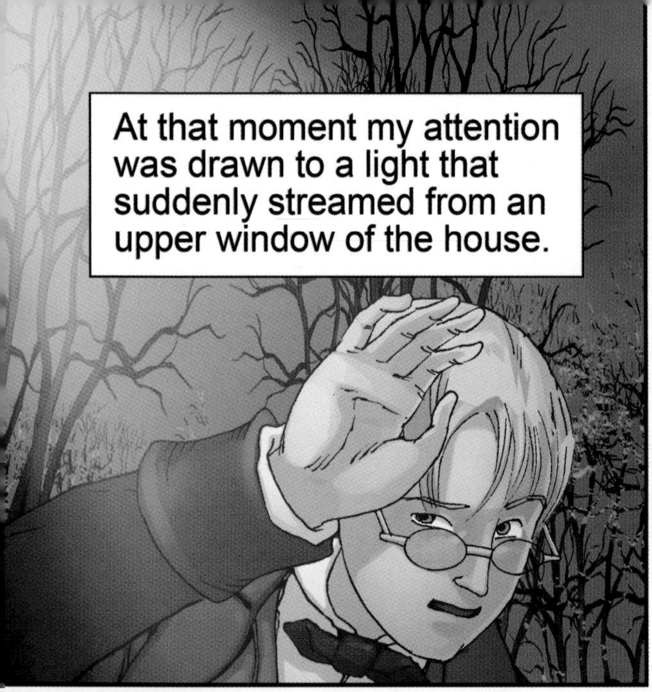
At that moment my attention was drawn to a light that suddenly streamed from an upper window of the house.

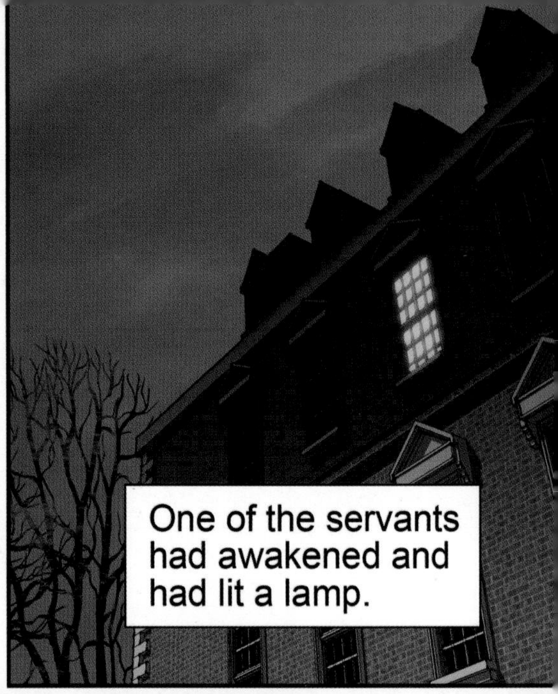
One of the servants had awakened and had lit a lamp.

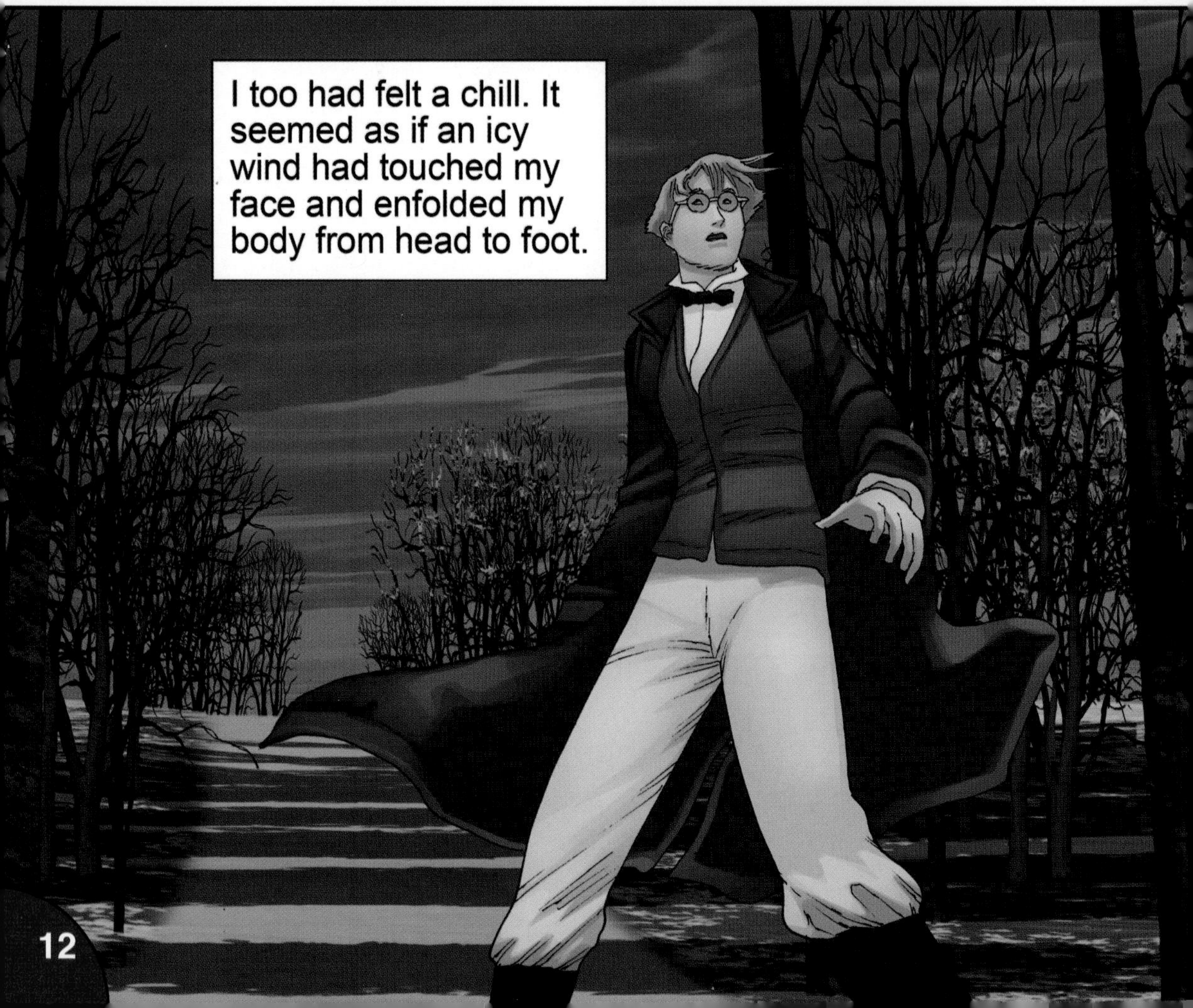
I too had felt a chill. It seemed as if an icy wind had touched my face and enfolded my body from head to foot.

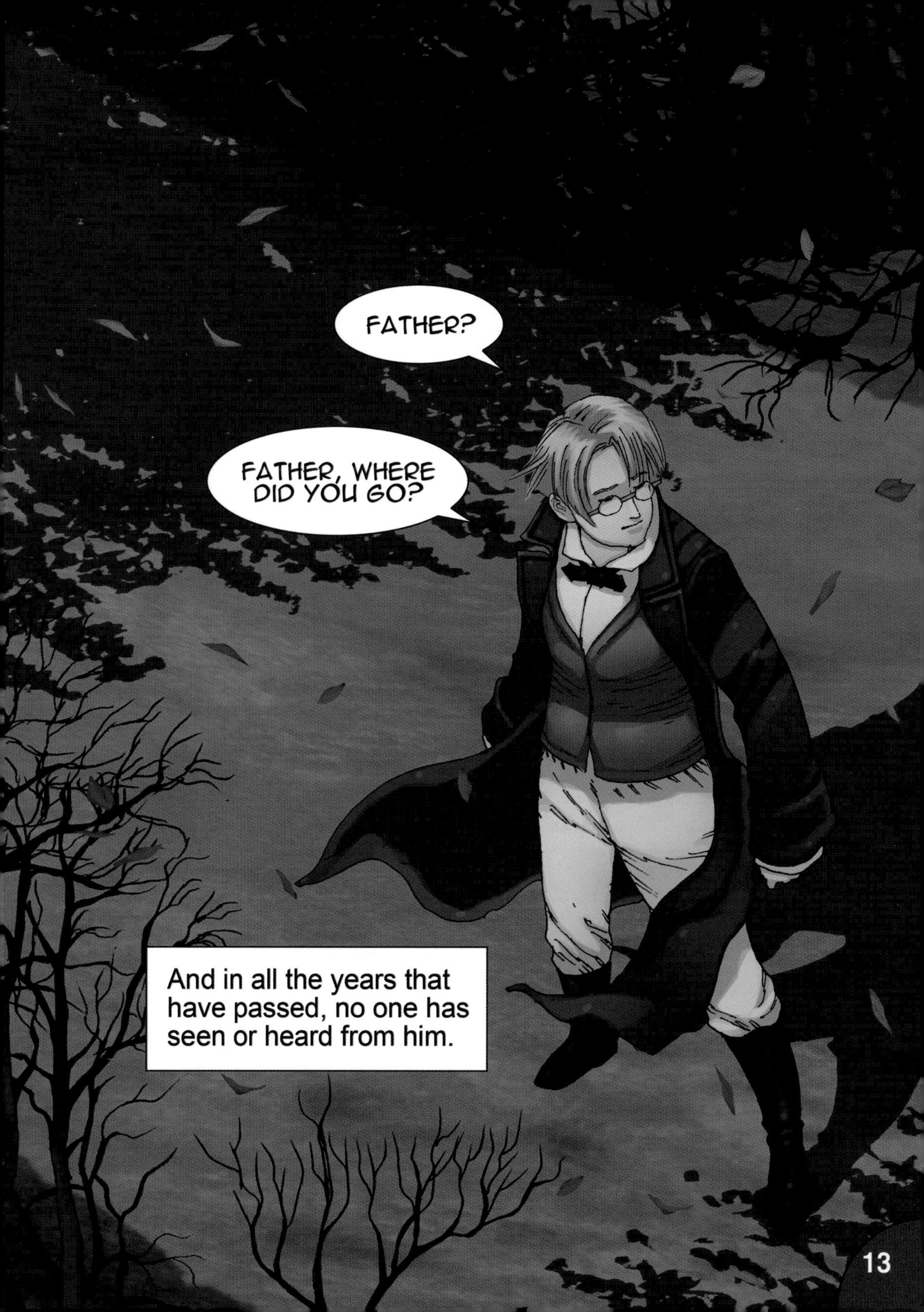
FATHER?
FATHER, WHERE DID YOU GO?
And in all the years that have passed, no one has seen or heard from him.

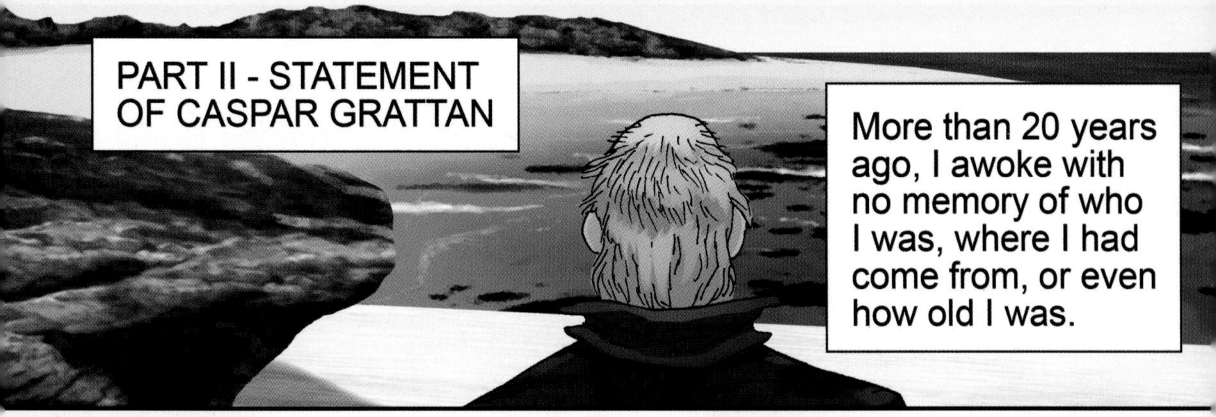
PART II - STATEMENT OF CASPAR GRATTAN
More than 20 years ago, I awoke with no memory of who I was, where I had come from, or even how old I was.

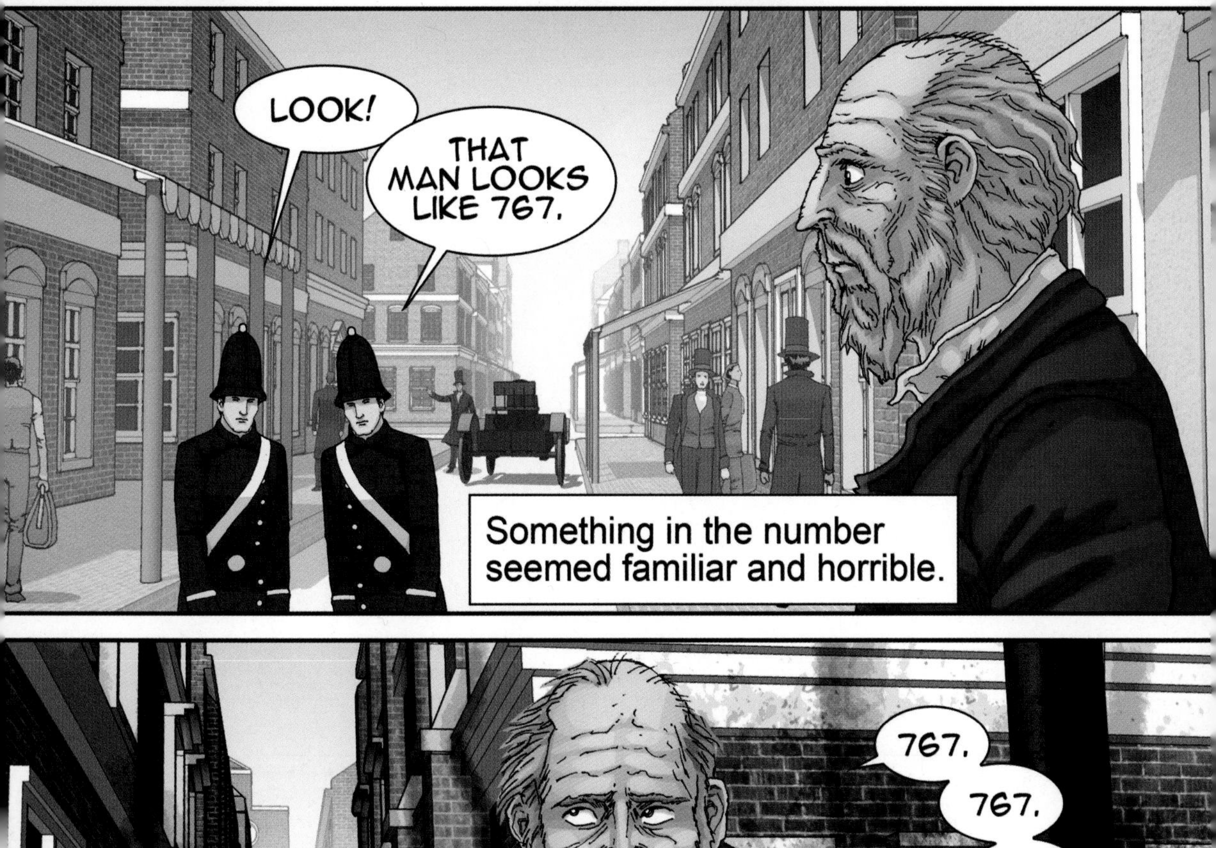
LOOK!
THAT MAN LOOKS LIKE 767.
Something in the number seemed familiar and horrible.

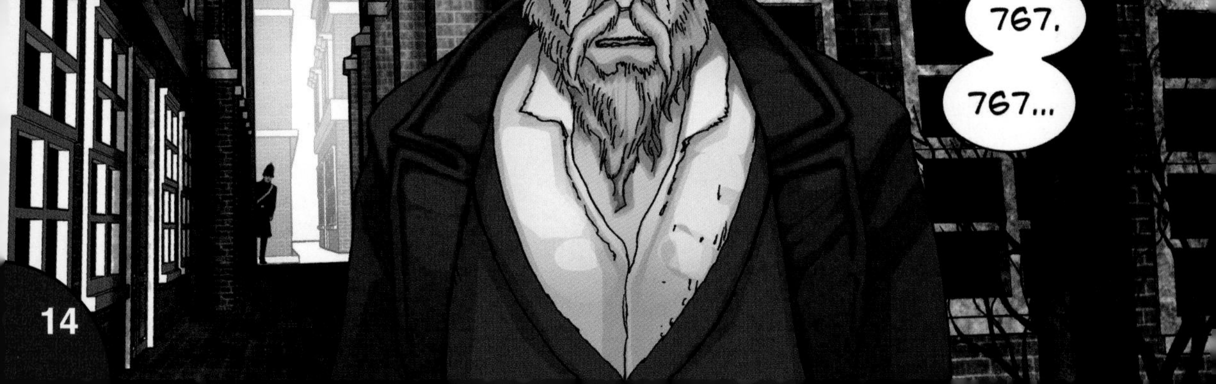
767.
767.
767.
767...

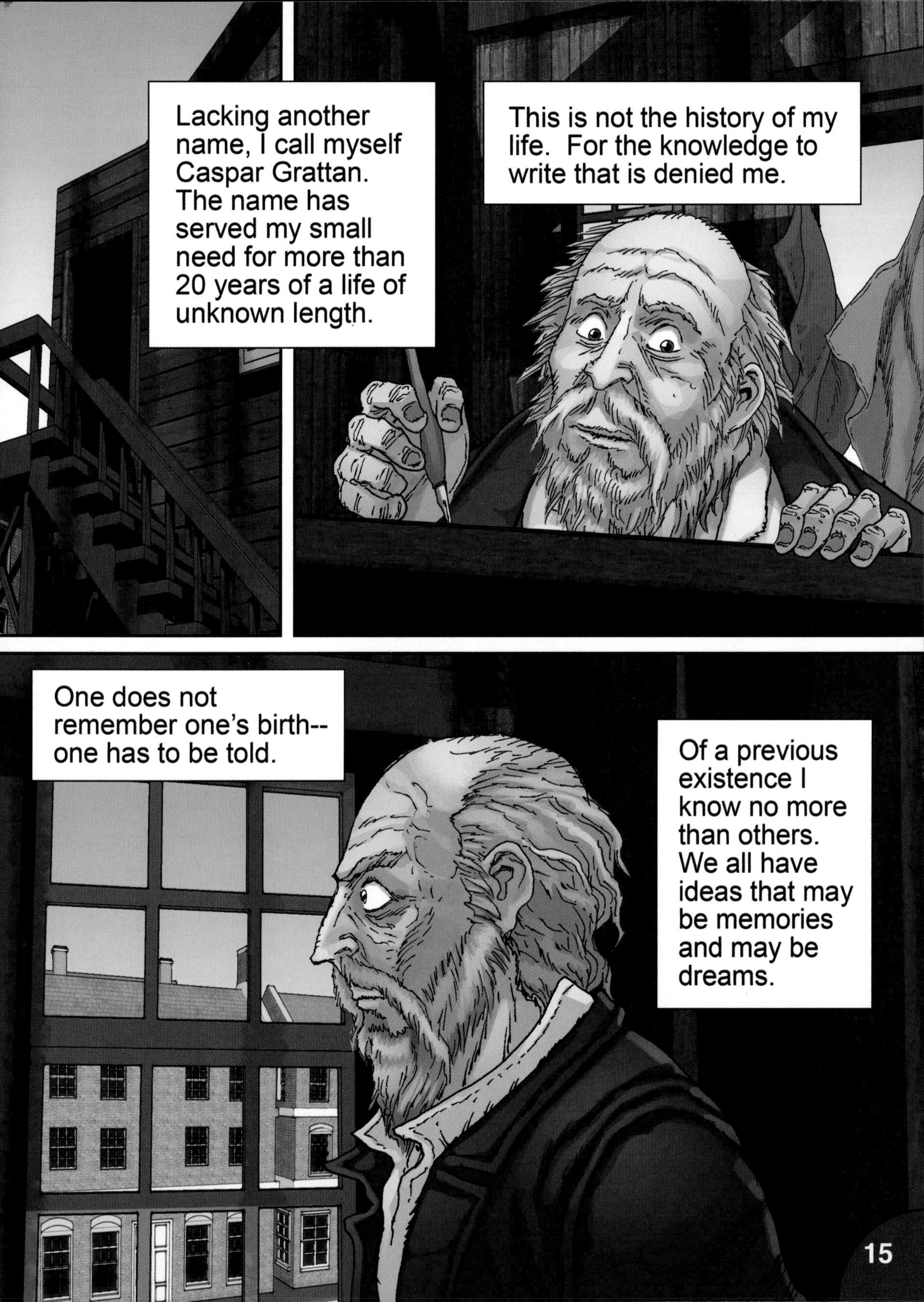

Lacking another name, I call myself Caspar Grattan. The name has served my small need for more than 20 years of a life of unknown length.

This is not the history of my life. For the knowledge to write that is denied me.

One does not remember one's birth-- one has to be told.

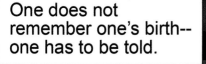

Of a previous existence I know no more than others. We all have ideas that may be memories and may be dreams.

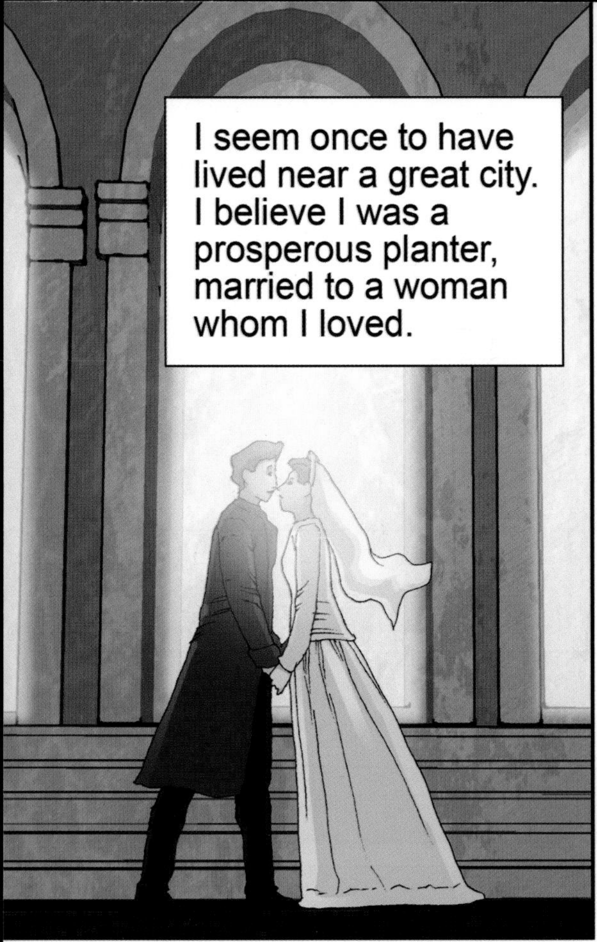
I seem once to have lived near a great city. I believe I was a prosperous planter, married to a woman whom I loved.

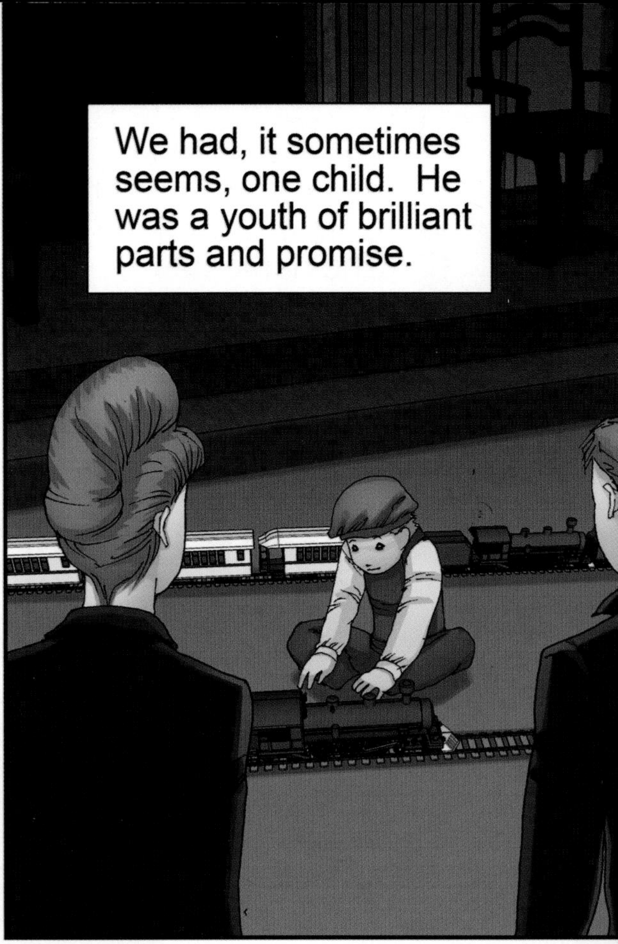
We had, it sometimes seems, one child. He was a youth of brilliant parts and promise.

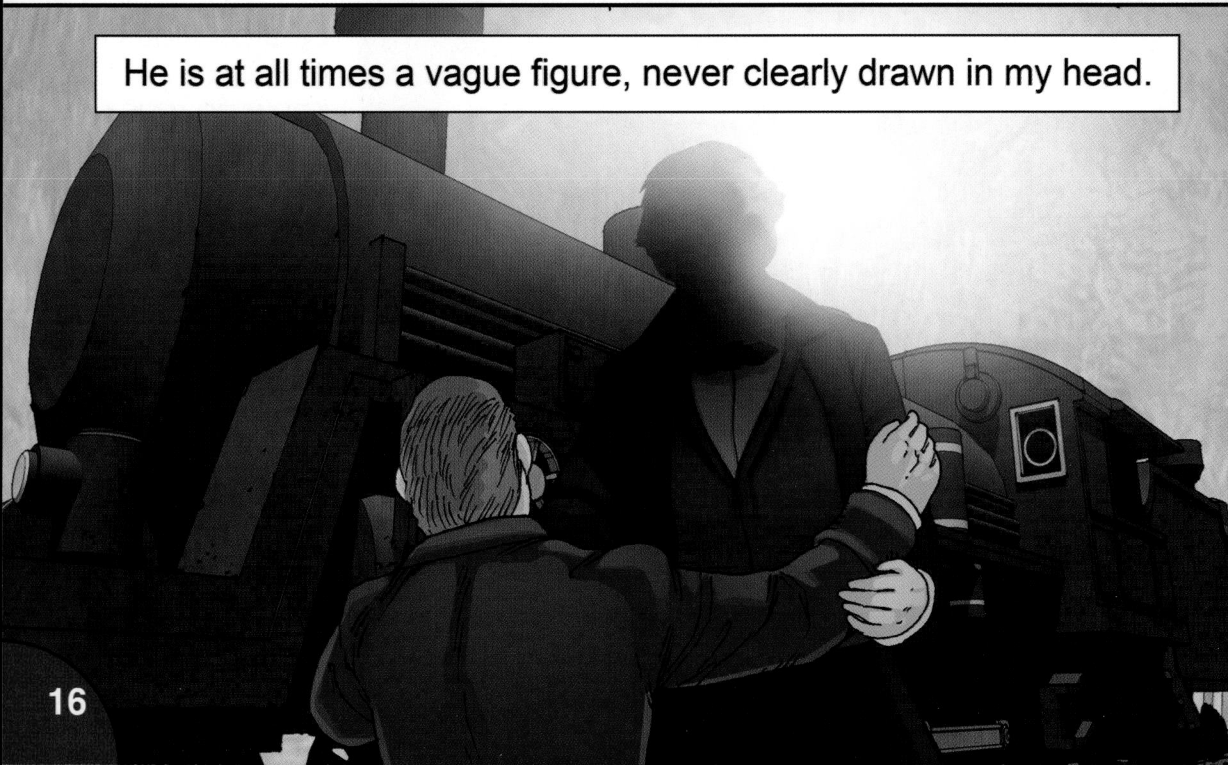
He is at all times a vague figure, never clearly drawn in my head.

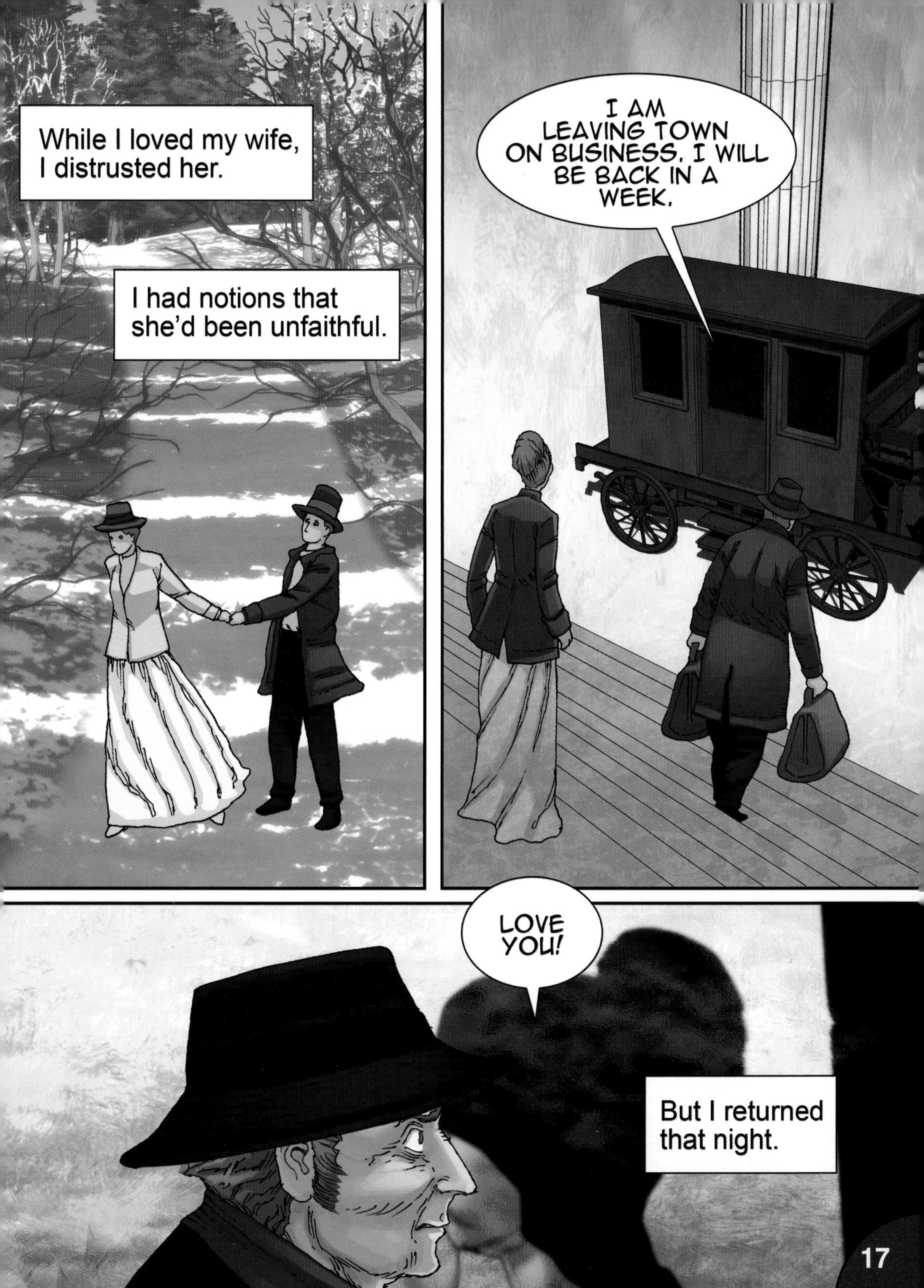
While I loved my wife, I distrusted her.
I had notions that she'd been unfaithful.
I AM LEAVING TOWN ON BUSINESS. I WILL BE BACK IN A WEEK.
LOVE YOU!
But I returned that night.

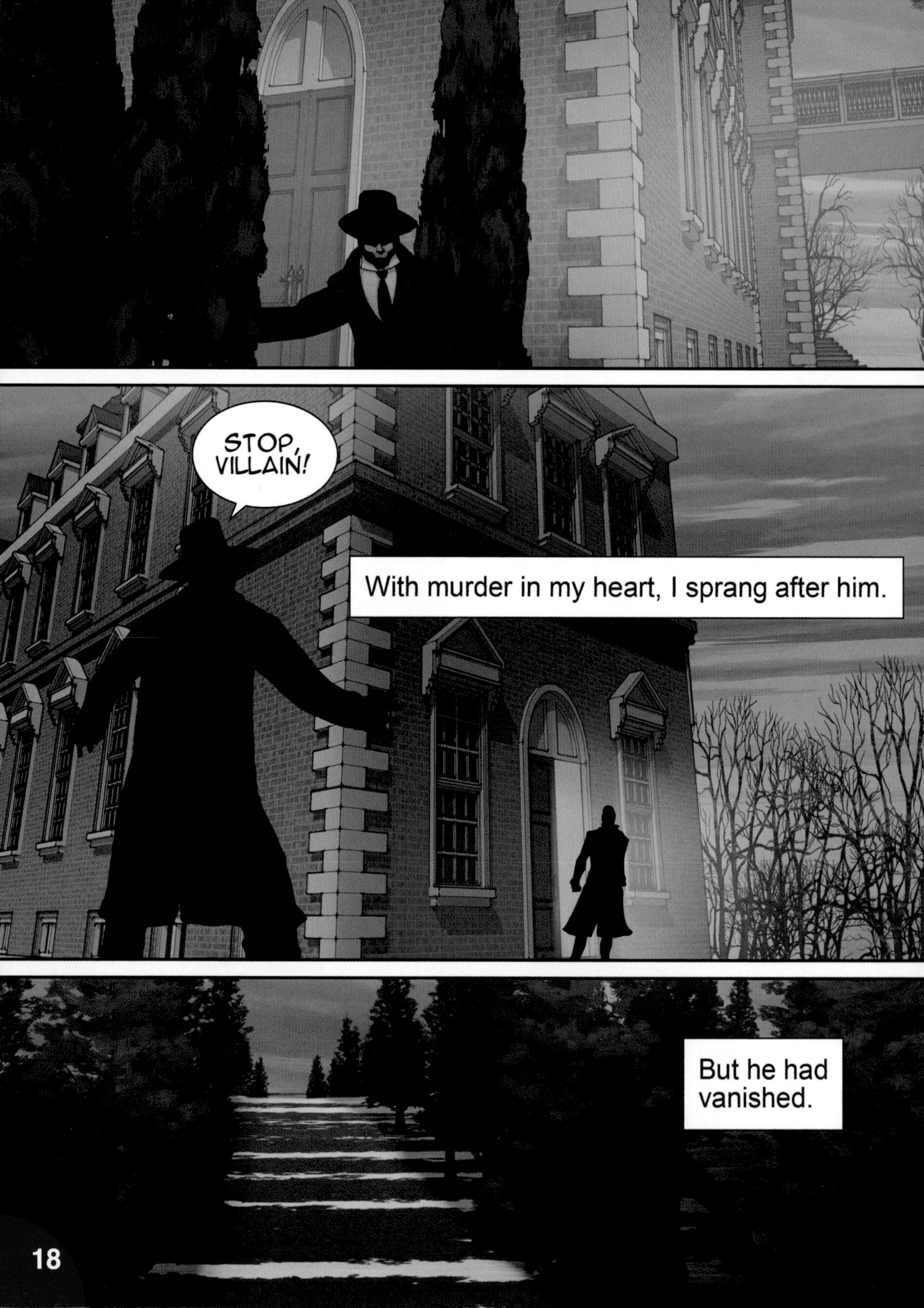
STOP, VILLAIN!
With murder in my heart, I sprang after him.
But he had vanished.

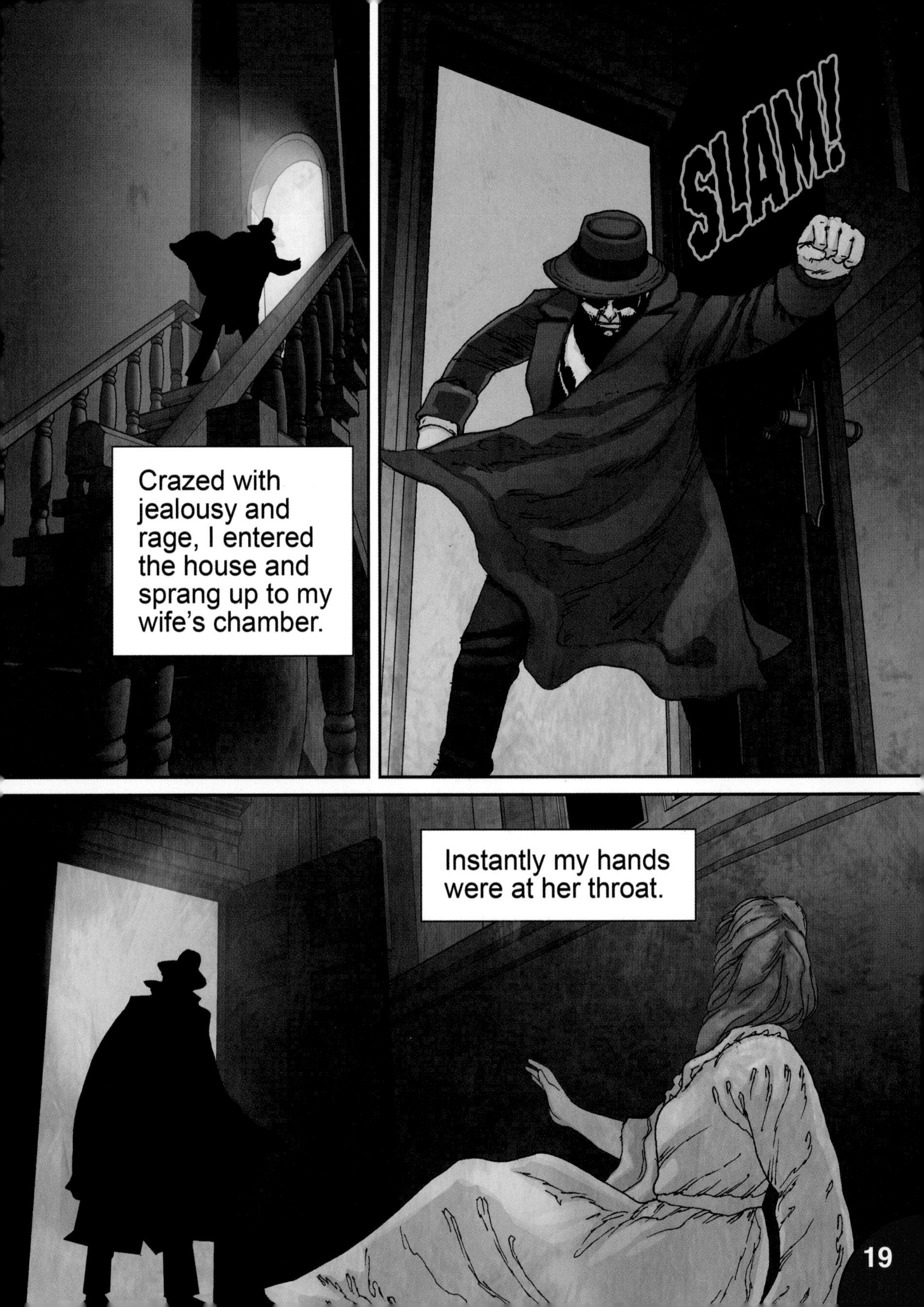
Crazed with jealousy and rage, I entered the house and sprang up to my wife's chamber.
SLAM!
Instantly my hands were at her throat.

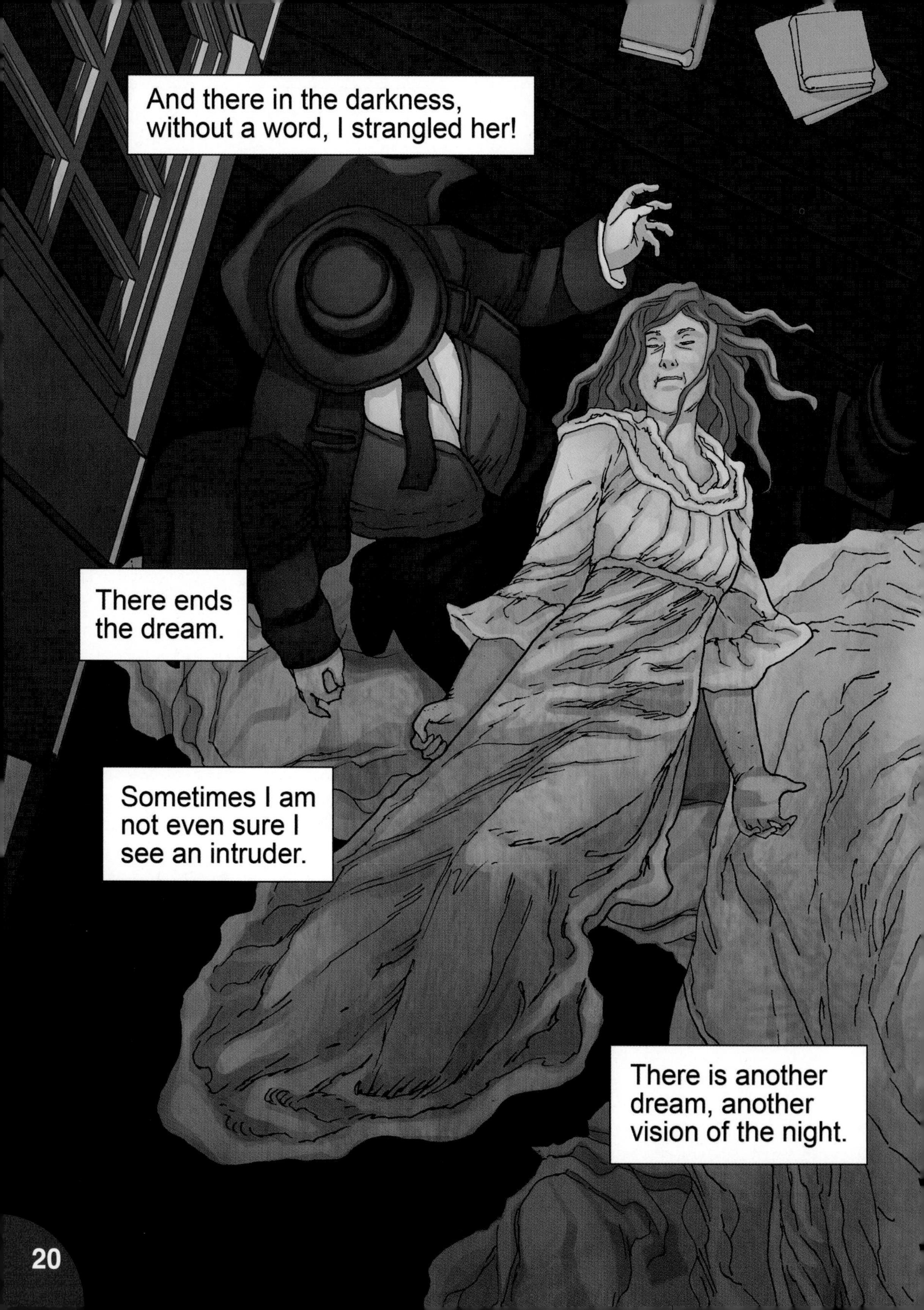
And there in the darkness, without a word, I strangled her!
There ends the dream.
Sometimes I am not even sure I see an intruder.
There is another dream, another vision of the night.

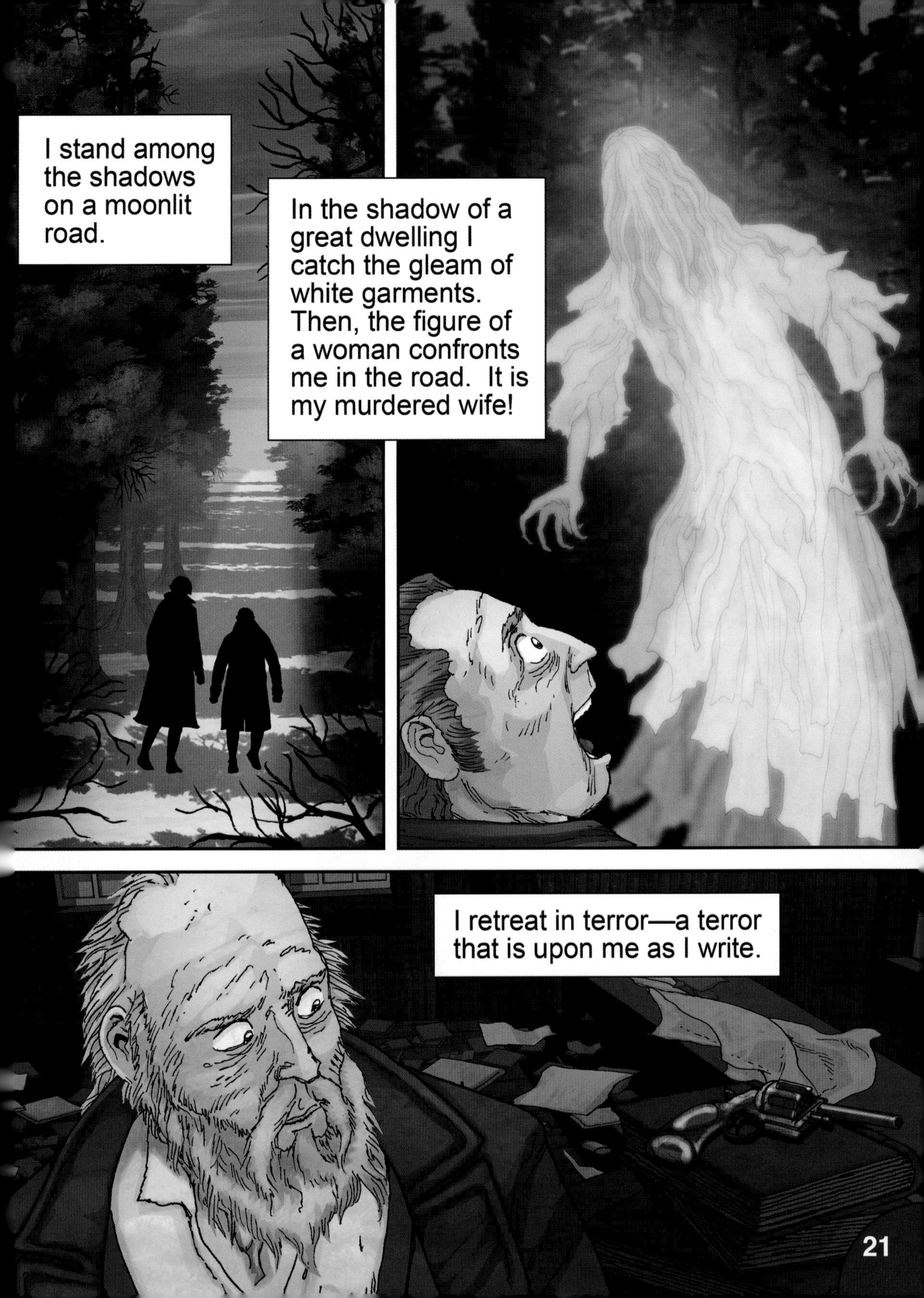
I stand among the shadows on a moonlit road.
In the shadow of a great dwelling I catch the gleam of white garments. Then, the figure of a woman confronts me in the road. It is my murdered wife!
I retreat in terror—a terror that is upon me as I write.

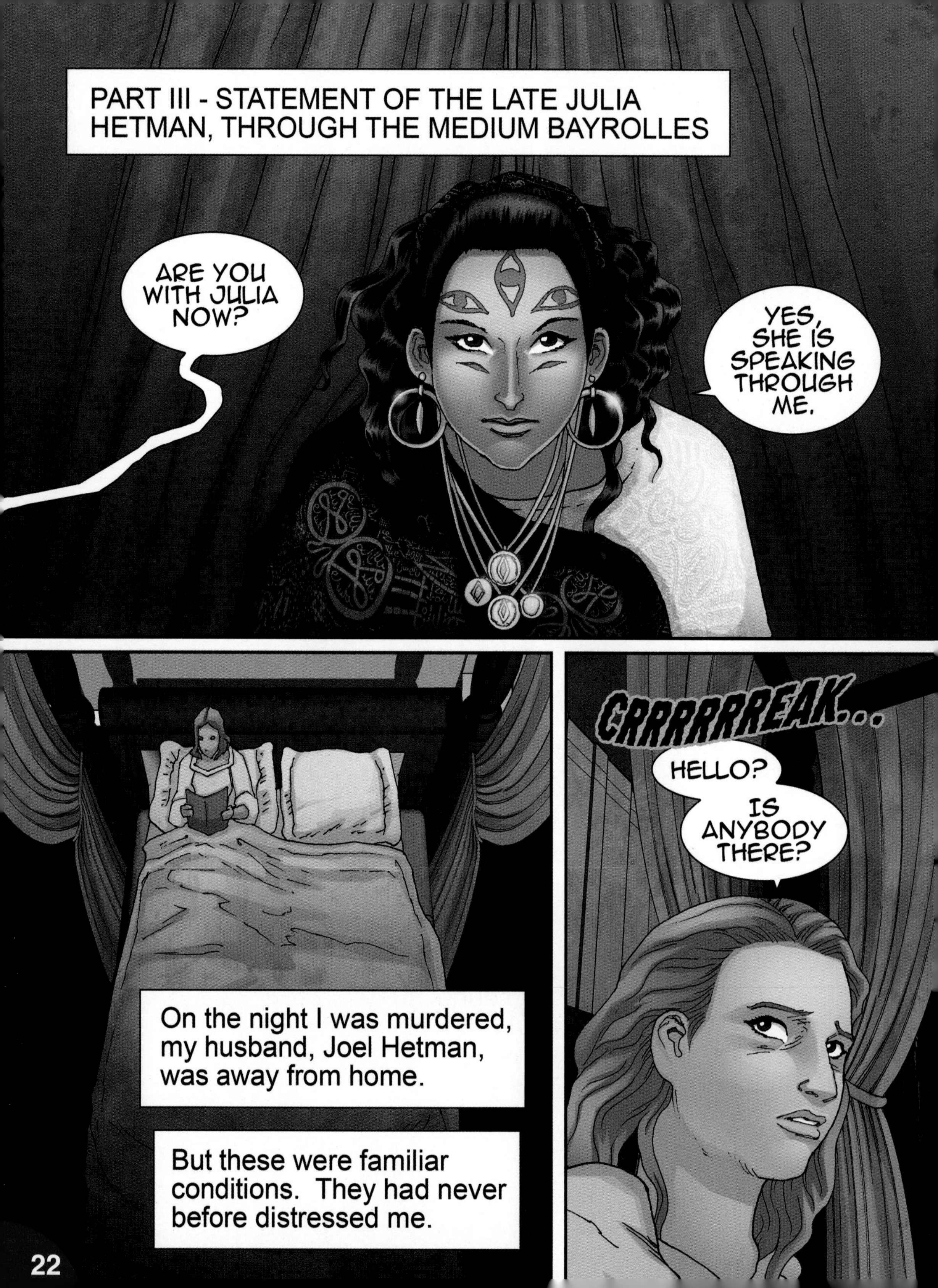
PART III - STATEMENT OF THE LATE JULIA HETMAN, THROUGH THE MEDIUM BAYROLLES
ARE YOU WITH JULIA NOW?
YES, SHE IS SPEAKING THROUGH ME.
On the night I was murdered, my husband, Joel Hetman, was away from home.
But these were familiar conditions. They had never before distressed me.
CRRRRRRREAK...
HELLO?
IS ANYBODY THERE?

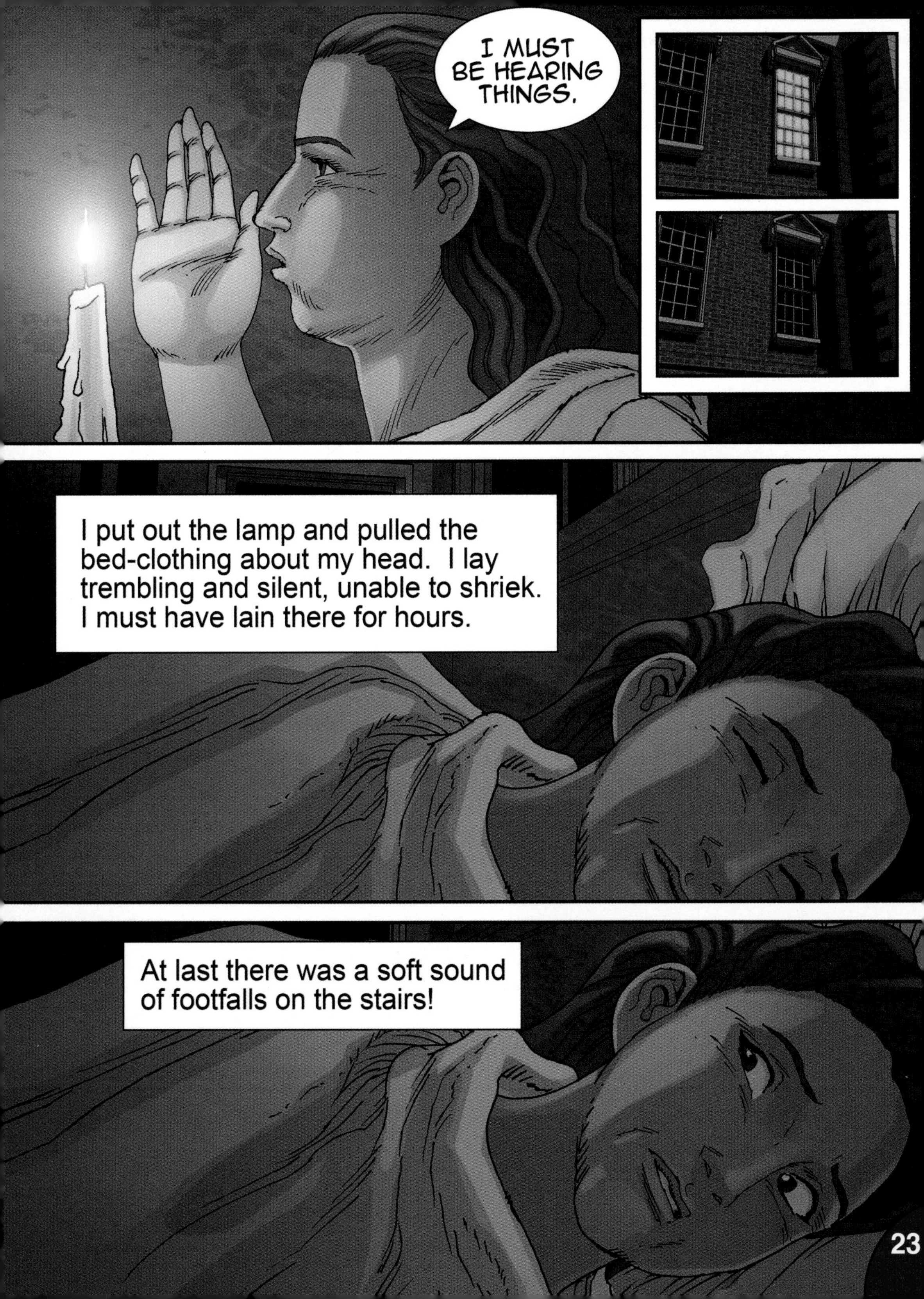
I MUST BE HEARING THINGS.
I put out the lamp and pulled the bed-clothing about my head. I lay trembling and silent, unable to shriek. I must have lain there for hours.
At last there was a soft sound of footfalls on the stairs!

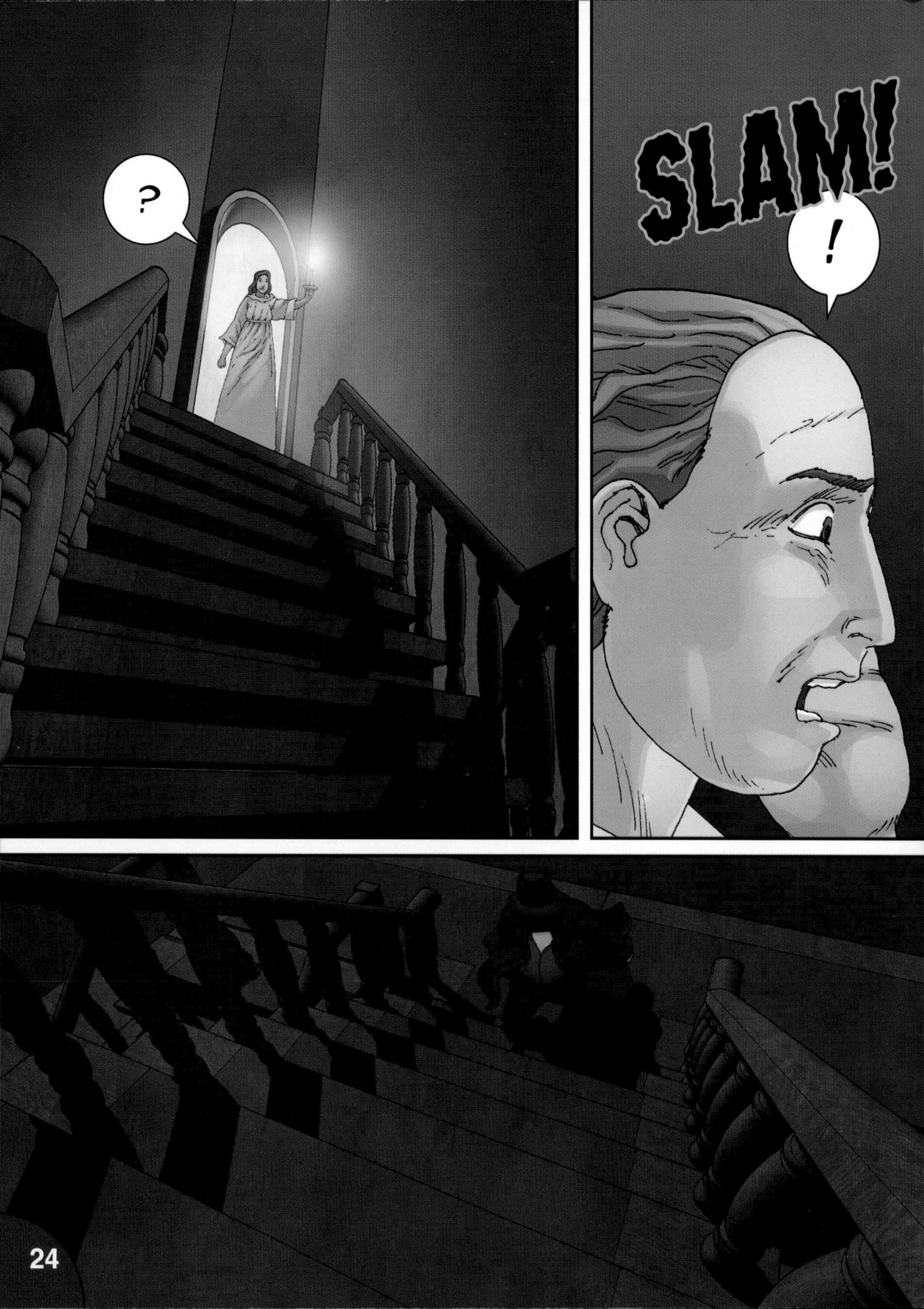
?
SLAM!
!

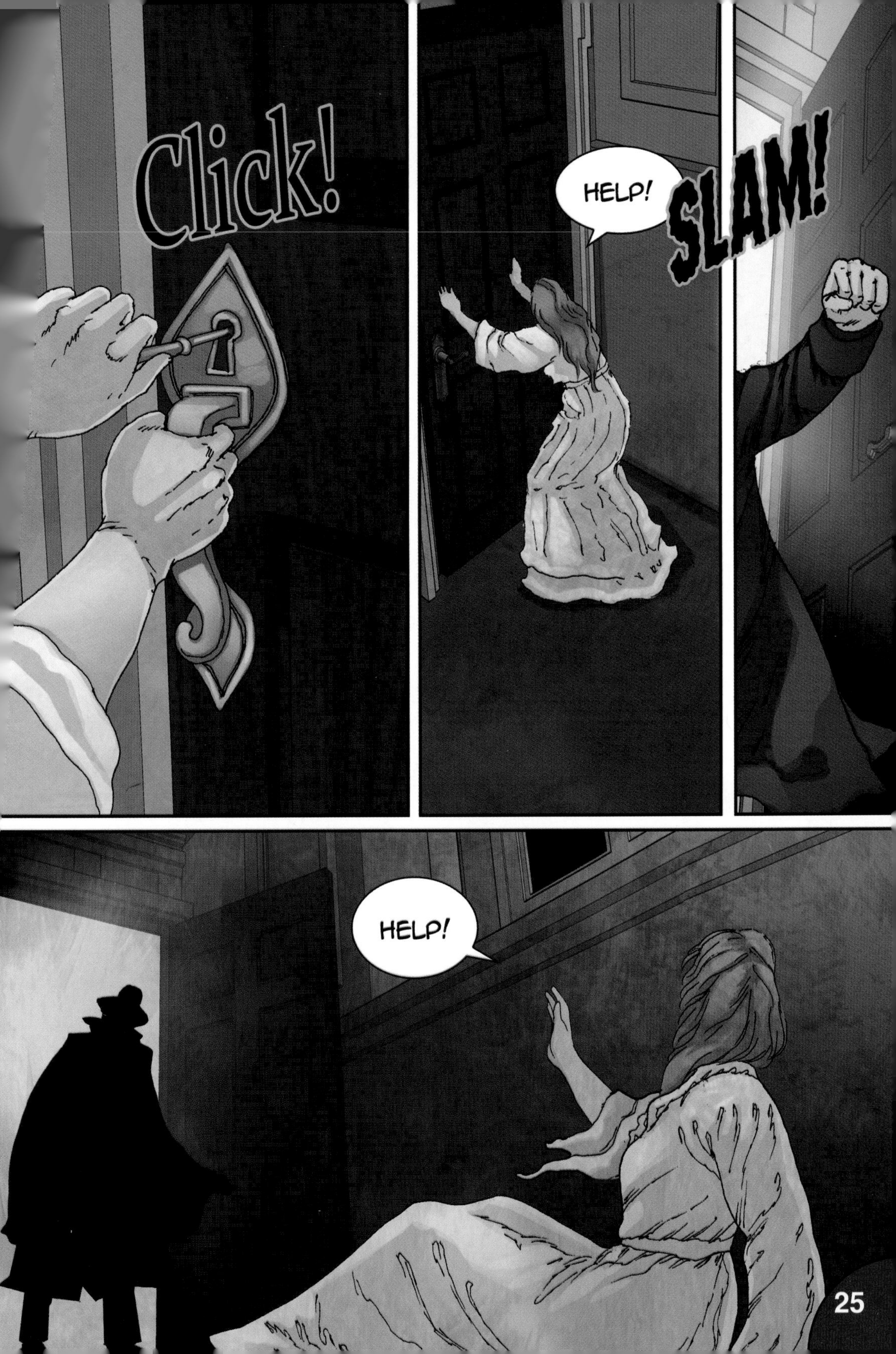
Click!
HELP!
SLAM!
HELP!

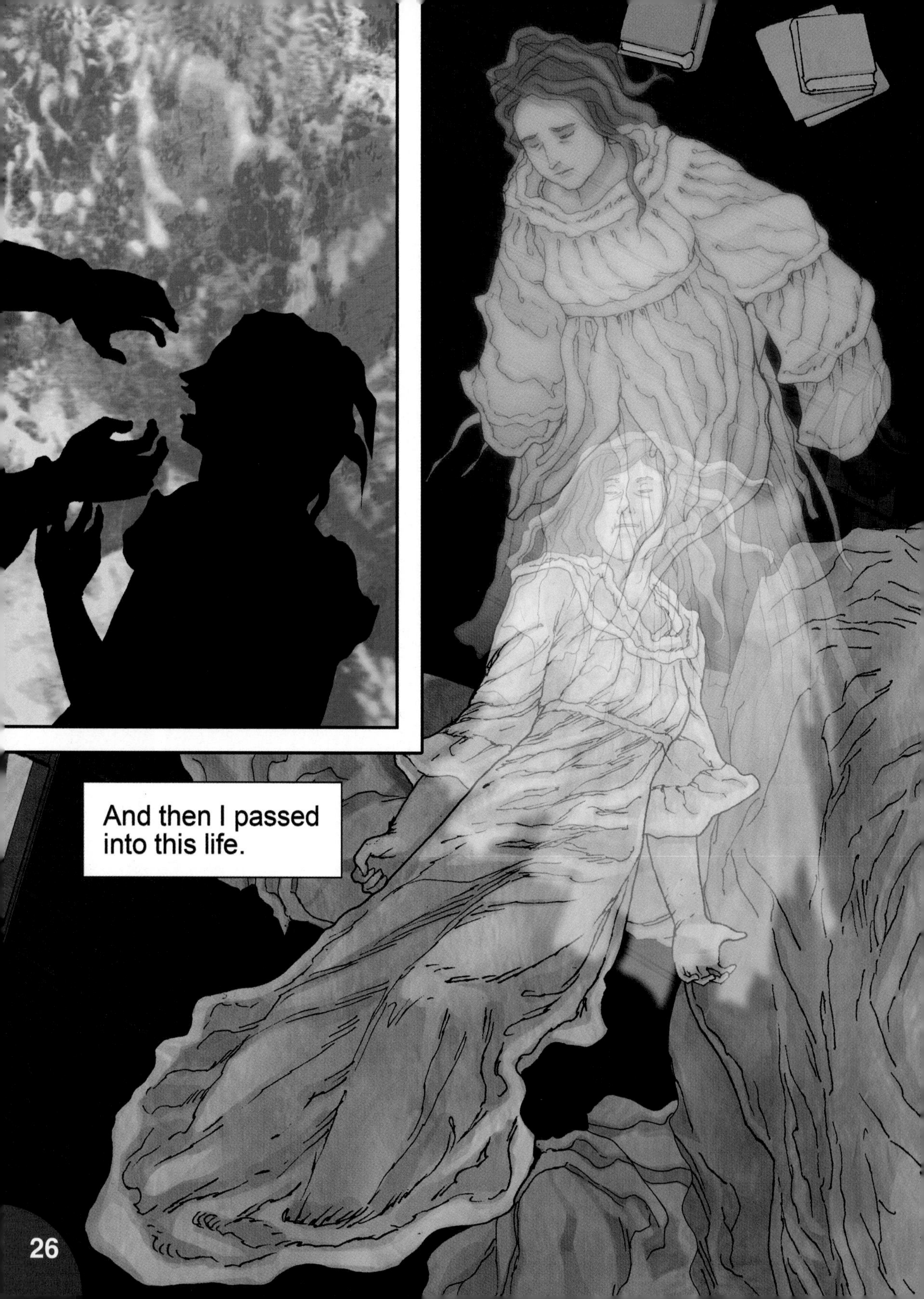
And then I passed into this life.

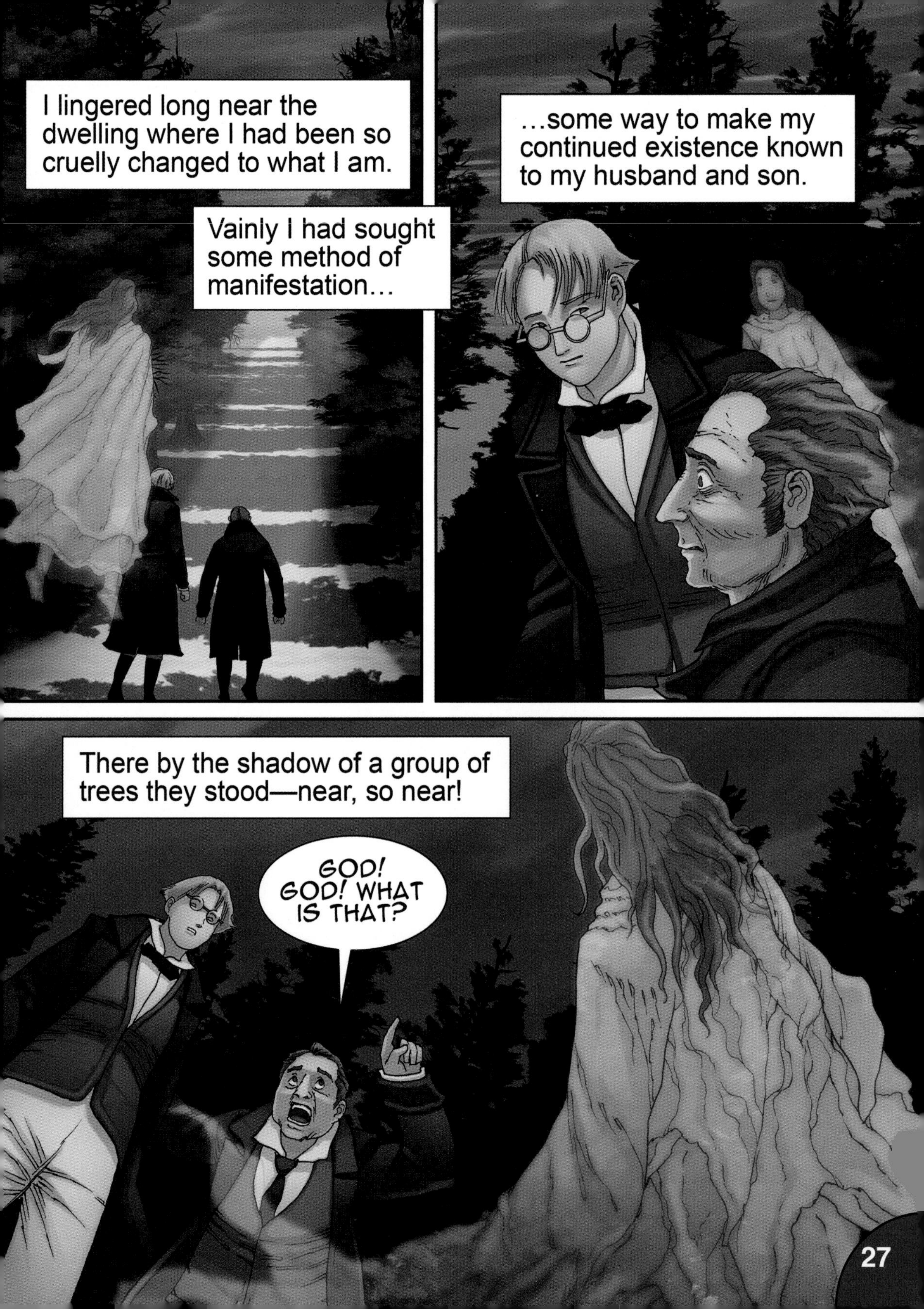
I lingered long near the dwelling where I had been so cruelly changed to what I am.
Vainly I had sought some method of manifestation…
…some way to make my continued existence known to my husband and son.
There by the shadow of a group of trees they stood—near, so near!
GOD! GOD! WHAT IS THAT?

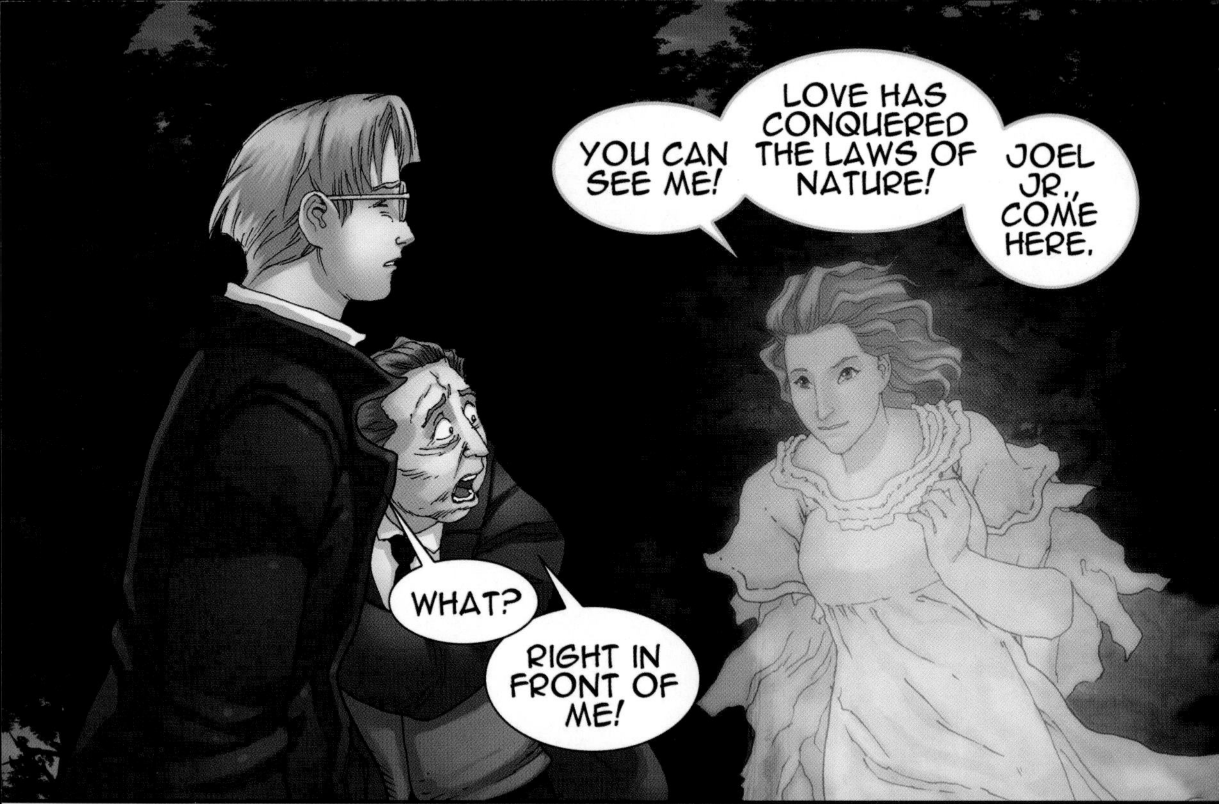
YOU CAN SEE ME!
LOVE HAS CONQUERED THE LAWS OF NATURE!
JOEL JR., COME HERE.
WHAT?
RIGHT IN FRONT OF ME!

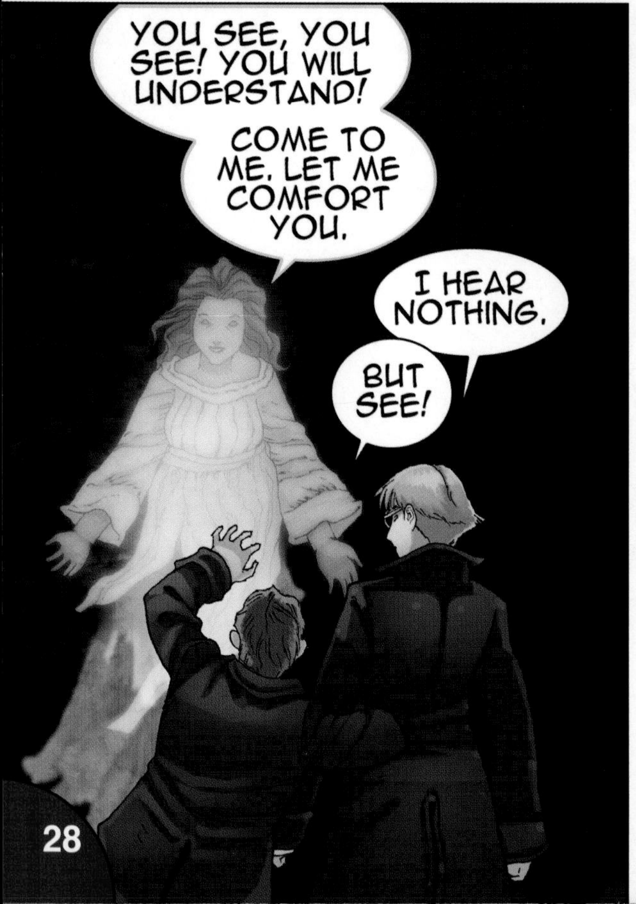
YOU SEE, YOU SEE! YOU WILL UNDERSTAND!
COME TO ME. LET ME COMFORT YOU.
I HEAR NOTHING.
BUT SEE!

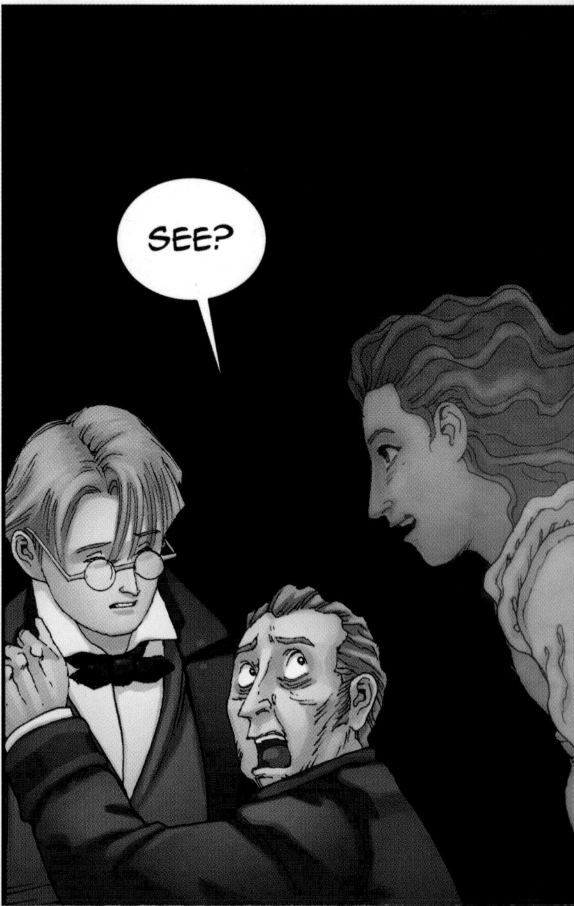
SEE?

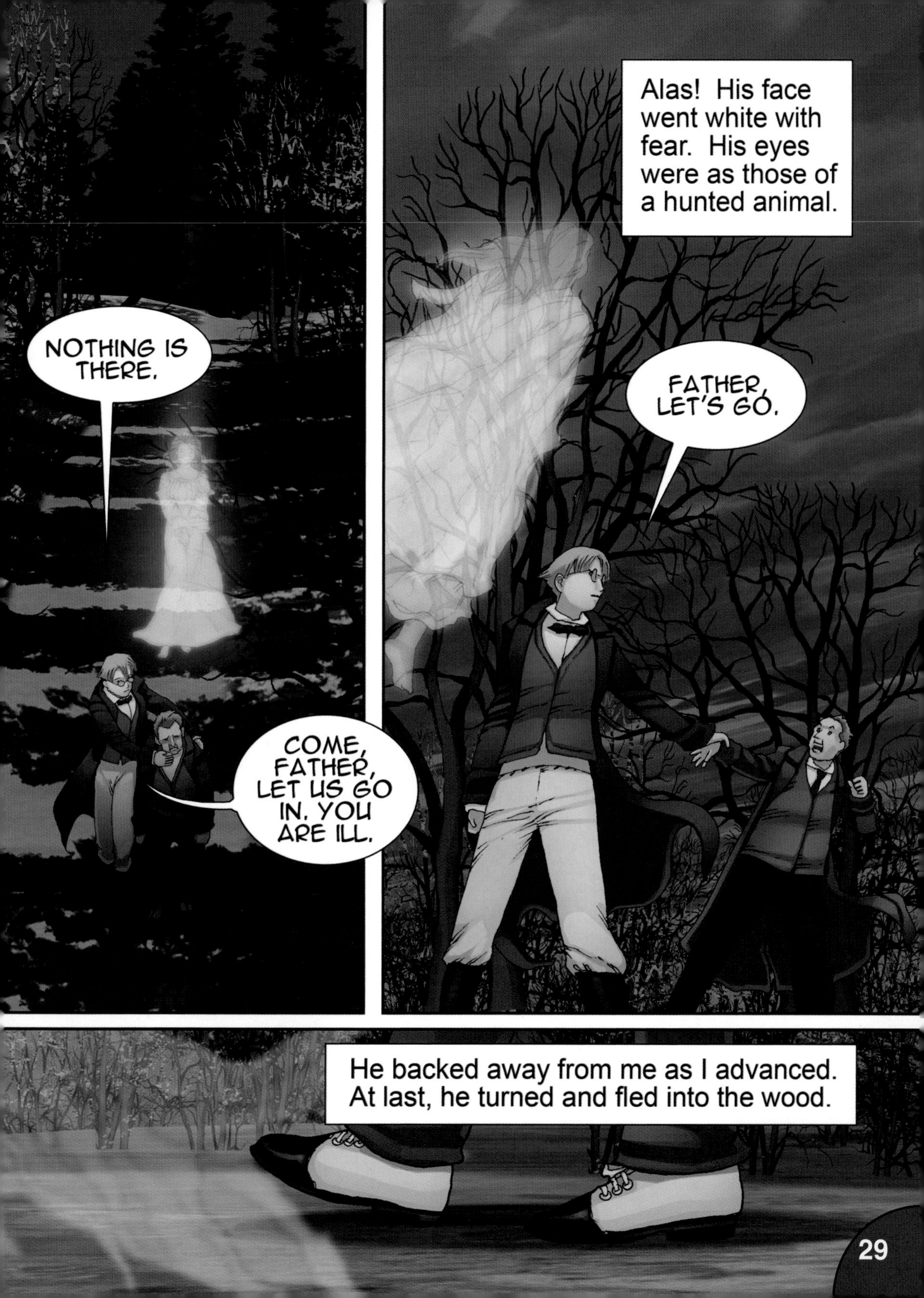
NOTHING IS THERE.
COME, FATHER, LET US GO IN. YOU ARE ILL.
Alas! His face went white with fear. His eyes were as those of a hunted animal.
FATHER, LET'S GO.
He backed away from me as I advanced. At last, he turned and fled into the wood.

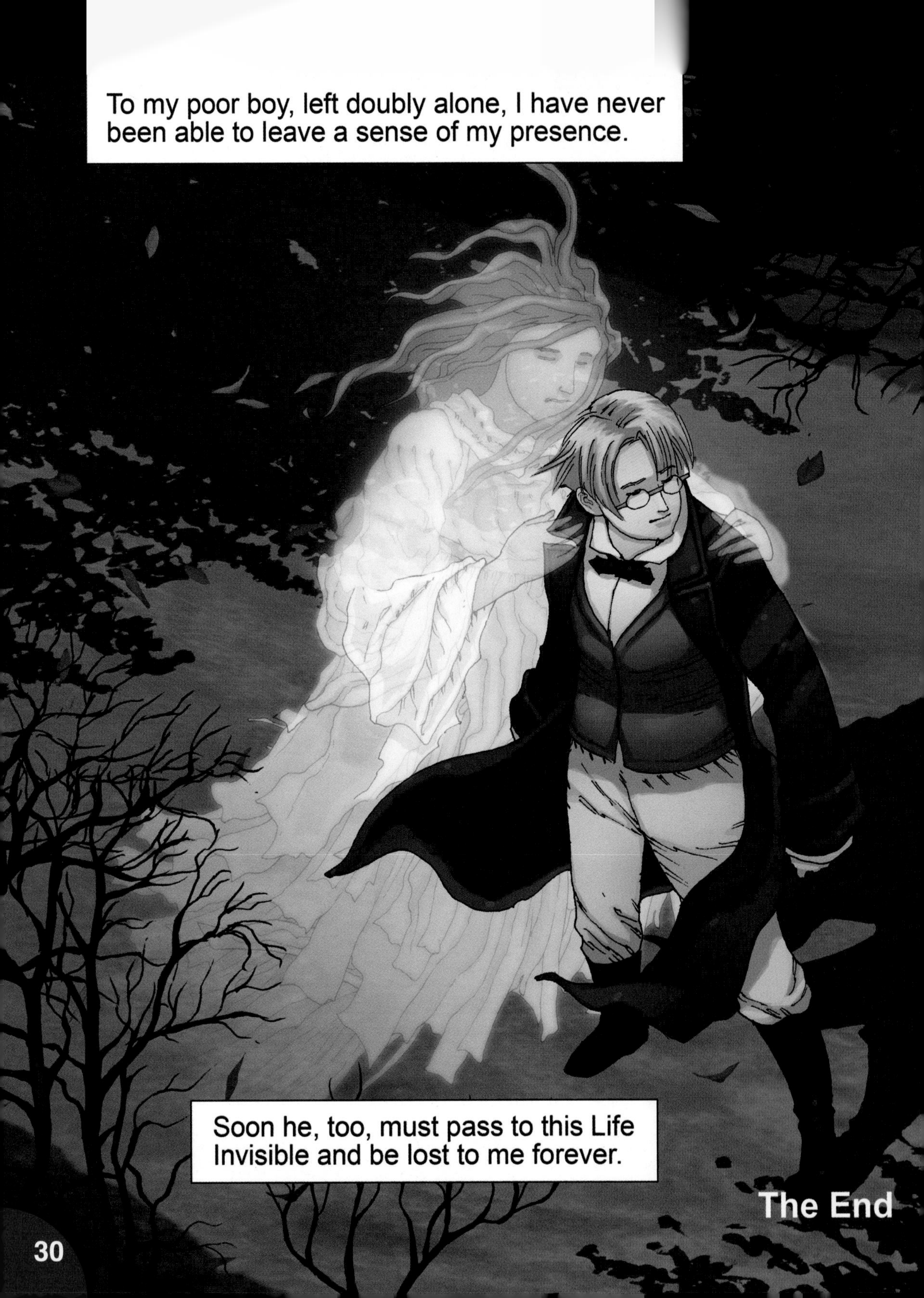
To my poor boy, left doubly alone, I have never been able to leave a sense of my presence.
Soon he, too, must pass to this Life Invisible and be lost to me forever.
The End

About the Author

Ambrose Gwinnett Bierce was born in Meigs county, Ohio, on June 24, 1842. Ambrose was raised in Indiana. After high school, he became a printer's apprentice on a newspaper in Warsaw, Indiana.

In 1861, Bierce enlisted in the 9th Indiana Volunteers. He fought in several Civil War battles. He was seriously injured in the Battle of Kennesaw Mountain in 1864. He served in the Civil War until 1865.

After the war, Bierce moved to San Francisco, California. He began writing for periodicals, including the *News Letter*. He became editor of the *News Letter* in 1868. In 1871, Bierce married Mary Ellen Day. Over the years, Bierce worked for many papers and magazines. He wrote several books as well as news stories and newspaper columns.

In 1913, Bierce went to Mexico. The end of his life is a mystery, but some believe he was killed in the siege of Ojinaga in January 1914. During his lifetime he had written many articles and short stories. However, it is through his Gothic stories of fear, death, horror, and the supernatural that he will be best remembered.

Additional Works

The Haunted Valley (1871)
The Fiend's Delight (1872)
Nuggets and Dust Panned Out in California (1872)
Cobwebs from an Empty Skull (1874)
In the Midst of Life (1892)
Can Such Things Be? (1893)
The Cynic's World Book (1906)

Glossary

assassin - someone who murders another.

dwelling - a shelter where people live.

footfalls - the sound of footsteps.

linger - to be slow to leave.

manifestation - a ghostly figure that becomes visible.

medium - a person who is said to communicate with the world of the spirits.

strangulation - to be killed by choking.

Web Sites

To learn more about Ambrose Bierce, visit the ABDO Group online at **www.abdopublishing.com**. Web sites about Bierce are featured on our Book Links page. These links are routinely monitored and updated to provide the most current information available.